SIN & SAINT

J.M. DABNEY

EXECUTIONERS BOOK 4

ISBN-13: 978-1-947184-16-9

CONTENTS

Dedication

To my Readers, who've stuck with me through Twirled, Brawlers, and the Executioners, thank you all. You'll never know how much your support means.

Author's Note

Prologue

Everyone saw him as the leader. The one who would throw down his life for his team, but he was in a different universe at Brawlers bar. His cousin, Scary, owned the place with his husbands, Tank and Elijah. The biggest and most dangerous man he'd ever met was at a corner booth with his arms around his men, and fuck, he was jealous. Camden Pelter raised his perspiring beer bottle to his mouth and took a long draw. He couldn't remember the last time he relaxed enough for a beer or simply to hang out.

He'd come here for an operation, and he was supposed to be right back out of town. That was two days ago. The Powers, Georgia, Sheriff had been into some shit. He came to town to help bring the corrupt fucker down before the racist and homophobic bastard tried to take out Scary's crew for good.

He and his cousin weren't on the best terms. The last time they'd butted heads, he'd locked Scary up, and their grandmother had nearly disowned him. When Scary and his crew went silent after the shooting of the Sheriff, he thought he was going to have to threaten Scary again, but Elijah had come to the rescue by brokering a bit of a deal. He did like his cousin's extremely handsome husband. How the fuck Scary got him, he didn't know and sure as fuck didn't understand it.

"Hey, handsome, can I get you another." Twitch leaned on the bar.

The tiny man was married to a beast named Crave. He'd never met a man he'd call beautiful in his life, but Twitch was so much so, it made him uncomfortable. He wasn't in the closet, but he didn't advertise. In his line of work, the testosterone and machismo went right along with the homophobia. He needed to depend on his team to have his back when shit went nuclear during operations. A split-second hesitation could end with a suit showing up to notify your next of kin.

"Your man already threatened my nuts if I even smiled at you, beautiful."

Twitch's super sweet and lovely smile was enough to make someone nauseous.

"How else will I make my tips if I don't seduce them with my overwhelming gorgeousness?"

"Darlin', even on your worse day you probably turn heads."

"You do know I'm married, right?"

"Doesn't mean I can't appreciate the view, ain't that right?"

He couldn't contain his smile at the sweet little blush that spread across Twitch's tanned cheeks. How a man married to Crave could still blush fucking shocked him. The kid was cute, and from what he'd seen, Twitch was genuinely sweet and caring. He didn't see that much anymore.

It was nice to flirt even if he knew the boy was taken.

"There's a few boys appreciating the fine form sitting in front of me right now."

"Doubt that."

Soft fingertips touched his stubble covered cheek and turned his head toward the stage. Executioners, they were the house band and made up of the roughest sons of bitches he'd ever met. That's when he noticed them, perfect and blond, even more beautiful than Twitch and they were staring right at him. He gripped Twitch's wrist with a gentle pressure and slowly lowered the man's hand to the bar.

"I don't do jailbait."

Just looking at them had his jeans fitting too fucking tight and he released Twitch to bring his attention back to his drink.

"Twenty-one isn't jailbait. Sin and Saint are grown men."

"Not grown enough for a forty-three-year-old man." He darted another glance at the stage, but luckily those two boys weren't looking at him. Fuck, but they had him thinking shit he shouldn't. Like if their blond hair would be as soft as it looked wrapped around his fist. He clenched his jaw and forced himself to look away.

"You old men pay too much attention to age or is your sexy ass still in the closet?"

"Would I be here if I was in the closet?"

"I don't know. Your cousin owns the place."

"I'm not in the closet, but I don't advertise either."

"Maybe you should. You're single."

3

"I like being single." The lie tasted bitter on his tongue. It wasn't that he minded being single, but his existence had become pretty lonely since his SWAT days. He didn't have the time to invest, and his undercover assignments didn't allow for time to spend with a partner. In his mind, that hadn't seemed fair to someone who could potentially mean a lot more to him than a casual hookup.

Twitch snorted. "Those glances at Sin and Saint say otherwise."

"Sin and Saint, don't they have real names?" Even though the names seemed perfect, he didn't like them, and he wasn't going to call his—nothing his was in this bar.

"Sin is Eric, and Ellison is Saint, but I don't think they answer to them. Last I heard their mom started calling them Sin and Saint too."

"I won't be calling them Sin and Saint."

"Does that mean you'll be calling them because they're headed this way. Good luck."

He nearly hollered for Twitch when the little man darted away. He was a grown ass man so he could handle two pretty boys. Their platinum blond hair tousled around their beautiful faces. Fuck, he caught sight of himself in the mirror behind the bar, and he looked old, well, ancient compared to them. The silver patch in his goatee stood out starkly and reminded him he wasn't in his twenties or even thirties anymore.

Just don't be an asshole, Camden, he ordered himself. His hand locked tight around the bottle as the most beautiful men he'd ever seen flanked him on either side. Their slim bodies pushing in beside him, and he instantly knew which one was Sin. The boy pressed in tight to his side, while Ellison, Saint, kept a bit of distance. In his peripheral, he noticed the innocent pink that stained

4

Ellison's cheeks and he wanted to reach for him. Chase the spreading color under the pads of his calloused fingers.

"Well, hello, sexy, you're new."

Eric's soft fingertips stroked up his bare arm only being stopped by the rolled cuff of his dress shirt. His stomach tightened.

"Camden."

"You're Scary's cousin."

Ellison's voice was softer than Eric's, and tinged with a hint of shyness that made him want to turn to him.

"Why don't you come home with us, Camden?"

"Why don't you go play with someone your own age, boy?"

He didn't know where the brusque tone came from, but he didn't want to be some notch for boys with Daddy issues. It was a rage in his abdomen. An emotion he'd never experienced before burned through his veins, and he couldn't think beyond getting as far away from Eric and Ellison as he could. Part of him wanted to put them over his knee for propositioning some strange man in a bar. The other part, the one he needed to rein in, wanted to take them home.

"Twitch," he called for the bartender and pulled enough from his pocket to cover his few beers, plus a generous tip.

"Goodnight, boys."

Eric looked at him like he was insane to turn them down and maybe he was, but he was a grown ass man, and he knew what he wanted. Ellison avoided glancing at him and instead of embarrassment or shyness, the young man looked ashamed. He pushed back from the bar and started to walk away.

"Goodnight, Camden."

Ellison's sweet voice called to him, and he imagined what it would sound like when the boy screamed his name as he was buried balls deep. Angry with himself, he strode toward the door.

He knew what he wanted, something or someone only his, someone to care for and make happy. A quick fuck he wasn't and twenty-one was too fucking young for what he had in mind. That didn't keep his mind from wandering to the twin temptations he'd left back at Brawlers, and it didn't disappear even as he drove in the opposite direction of Powers, Georgia, and from the things he knew he couldn't have.

1 Pelter Had to Be Strong

Two Years Later...

Powers Sheriff's Department was deserted, and the cells downstairs were empty. Camden stood outside, his uniform shirt sticking to his skin from the late Summer humidity and he watched Heidi's Diner across the street. The place was packed with the Crews, the men and women he felt he'd become friends with over the last year or so since he'd left his job with the Georgia State Police. He missed his team and the constant chaos, but the small-town pace had its charm too.

The Brawlers, Twirled World Ink, and Executioners Crews, along with Trenton Security laughed. He kept up his internal debate about whether to walk over and join them there, but the sight of two of the group forced him to stay away. Sin and Saint Gant set their sights on him before he'd even taken over the job there.

The night at Brawlers they'd come up to him and invited him home still clear in his mind. The invite had pissed him off, but part of him had regretted not taking them up on the offer. They were beautiful, and he'd wanted them from the moment his gaze fell on them across the Brawlers' barroom. His resolve quickly eroded the longer he was around them. They'd crashed out at his place the night of King and Linc's wedding. He'd watched them sleep. Tucking the blankets around them every time they'd slipped. They'd been so beautiful cuddled up together, but so damn young.

They'd never want what he had in mind for them. Fuck, he didn't even know what he wanted. His brain swirled in a chaotic maelstrom of fucking them into his mattress and also having them in his house—curled up with them on the couch. All that couple shit he'd avoided in the past.

Going home to an empty house killed him every night, and that hadn't been an issue before. He hung around the station, made excuses to himself, but it all came down to he didn't want to go home alone anymore. That meant giving in, but he had to be strong. The weight of the twenty-two-year age difference still caused him to feel like a dirty old man. There was almost the same difference in age between his friend Bull and the man's husband, Gregory. If anything, Bull and Gregory proved it could work.

Ellison, Saint, was beautiful with an innocence that called to him. His baby blue eyes seemed to be haunted by a past no one talked about. Eric, Sin, always had an in your face attitude. Fearless, yet vulnerable at the same time. He wanted to take care of them. Make sure they were always happy and content. They were blond, blue-eyed and femme. His temporary partners in the past were as muscular and masculine as him. Sex always seemed like a fight for dominance.

He jumped as his phone rang. He tugged his from his pocket and connected the call. "Pelter."

"Camden, must you always answer the phone that way. It doesn't show proper breeding."

He mentally groaned at his mother's voice. Sheri Pelter was probably still in her business finery, perfect from her styled black hair to her thousand-dollar suit to her stilettos. She'd be sipping her pre-dinner martini and waiting on the housekeeper to set the table.

"Hello, Mother. I thought it was a work call. How are you and Father?"

His father probably had his secretary bent over his desk as he pounded one out before coming home. His mother didn't care about his father's affairs as long as they lived the perfect lie at the country club.

"He phoned to say he was just about to leave the office."

Of course he did. Camden kept his snark in check. He promised himself to always be monogamous—he wouldn't be like his parents.

"What do I owe for the unexpected call?"

"I know Christmas is months away, but I wanted to make sure that you would be home this year. I know you spent last year with Eugene."

He bit his lip to keep from snorting at Scary being called Eugene. He'd mention that next time he saw his beast of a cousin. But the disgust in her voice tempered his amusement.

Over the years, he'd compared himself to his cousin. Camden's father and Scary's mother were half-siblings. Scary took after his mother, but Camden got his dark complexion from his mother. Everyone was shocked to find out they were related when he'd come to town. They really looked nothing alike.

"I don't know. I'd have to make sure to have a replacement, and Wren has husbands and a family at home. The rest of the deputies do too."

"They work for you, Camden. I expect you to come home. I'll need you home early so that we'll have time to fit you for an acceptable suit. Also, make sure you shave."

He brought his hand up to tug at his long goatee. It was a leftover from his undercover days. He couldn't remember the last time he was without facial hair. He'd also spent a months' pay on the last suit he'd bought. After forty-five years, it didn't come as a surprise his parents found him lacking since they had from him enlisting to taking a job as a small-town Sheriff.

"Could I bring a date?"

"Will your date be female?"

"You know it wouldn't be." He gritted his teeth and dropped his head back. He'd come out the day before he'd enlisted. He was told they didn't care who he fucked as long as he didn't flaunt it, but he knew they expected him to bring home a wife and breed the next generation of Pelters.

"Then I'll have to decline an invite of a guest."

Wouldn't his snobby mother love to know his current interest consisted of not one man but two? He could already anticipate the meltdown, she wouldn't do it in public because that would be vulgar behavior, but she'd make him and his date or dates pay dearly behind closed doors. He was almost tempted to see if he could find a male date, maybe not the twins. Yet Little, one of Linus' guys was a troublemaker, would jump at the chance to crash a country club Christmas dinner. The thought of it amused him more than it should and way too tempting.

"Yes, ma'am."

He didn't want to fight, so he let it go.

"Your father just arrived. I'll let you return to your duties, and I expect you to inform me of when you'll arrive for the holidays."

She disconnected the call without a bye or an I love you. Camden shoved his phone back into his pocket. When he thought back on his life growing up, he couldn't remember either of his parents saying they were proud of him or that they loved him. He'd received all that from his paternal grandmother. He missed her. She'd taken care of him and Scary. While Scary had a loving parent, all he'd had was disinterested ones, but a loving grandmother. She'd given him all the love he had ever needed until she was gone and he was back to being that ignored rich kid. Envied for what he had, but wouldn't all those jealous fucks loved to have known just how miserable it was being him.

His stomach growled, and he snarled. He debated whether to just grab something from the vending machine inside or go out to the highway to grab some fast food.

He groaned, there was a perfectly good restaurant across the damn street. Two pretty little blonds weren't going to make him run like a goddamned coward. No matter how big of one he was. He was terrified, and he was going to give in, he just wondered how long he could hold out.

He crossed the deserted street and walked straight into chaos. Everyone called his name and waved, and Heidi nodded and went to put in his usual order. He loved it there no matter how lacking his parental units found him.

2 Being Good Was a Drag

This was the life, Eric *Sin* Gant thought to himself as he stocked another row of ten-inch Caucasian toned dildos. The store he co-managed with his twin, Ellison, was simply called Pleasure. Three years of employment bliss, it was a dream job, and the best part was he got to work every day with his twin. Even if the little shit was as straight-laced as Ellison could get. There was a reason Ellison was called Saint. Being good was such a drag though. He left that bullshit to Saint.

He grabbed the display model and headed for the counter where Saint was huddled over his laptop doing the weekly accounting.

"Saint," he called his brother's name and was ignored. "Saint," he repeated as he tapped his zoned-out brother's cheek with the tip of the dong. "Saint, are you listening to me?" he drew out the last word until he had to catch his breath. He giggled as he smacked Saint harder with the silicone.

Saint slapped at the silicone. Sin watched his twin's ice-blue eyes widen and then narrow.

"What the fuck do you...asshole, fucking stop!"

"Take a break."

"No. Fred wants all this done for tomorrow, and I can't play with the toys all day like you. I have to upload the new merchandise to the website."

"You know what toy I want to play with, but you won't let me attack him!"

"What is it I keep telling you about handcuffs and police records?"

"That it sounds like a party?" He smirked as Saint rolled his eyes. "Just because you're all goody-goody and won't join me in the kidnapping plot of having a hot Sheriff handcuffed to our bed, doesn't mean I've given up on the idea."

"Have you forgotten we're a hundred and thirty pounds and too pretty for jail?"

"I'm not the one with the Biker Daddy Fetish, but the morals of an eighty-year-old nun."

"I don't have the morals of a nun. He doesn't like us, Sin, or didn't he make that clear enough when we asked him out?"

"He just doesn't know what he's missing."

"He practically ran from us."

Ah fuck, he hated when his twin was sad because they fought a lot, but that's just what they did. Their mother said they'd been fighting since conception. Saint was always the quieter and shyer of them. Their teen years were hell on Saint. Although, he'd tried his damnedest to make it as happy as possible for Saint. They'd tried modeling, but Saint always had an issue with losing weight, and took the brunt of nasty comments about some non-existent, okay, not to non-existent muffin top. So his twin didn't have zero body fat, there wasn't anything wrong with that.

"We just have to make him see us as mature."

Saint arched a perfectly groomed brow, and he couldn't help cackling as he noticed he was waving the dildo around as he talked.

"Mature, when have we ever been seen as mature?"

"It's just a fucking thought."

Saint jerked the toy out of his hand and slammed it down on the counter, and the suction cup caught. It swayed a few times before settling.

"Well, forget about it. I have to—"

The obscene moaning coming over the PA system signaled they had a customer. They both looked toward to the door and groaned in unison as the object of their obsession walked into the main room. Two-hundred-fifty pounds of prime, mature male in a Sheriff's uniform swaggered in. His dark chestnut skin, perfection.

A well-aimed smack to the back of his head made him growl.

"Wipe the fucking drool," Saint ordered. "Hello, Sheriff Pelter, what can we do for you today?"

"Cock rings, anal beads, we just got in—"

"Shut up," Saint muttered under his breath.

"Eric, Ellison." The Sheriff's voice was like rough silk. It was a voice meant for dirty talk.

"We've told you to call us Sin and Saint."

Camden ignored them and continued on, "Your neighbor came to see me again this morning."

"She shouldn't be looking in our windows."

"I don't think your stained-glass window installation in the backyard technically qualifies as your windows."

"Naked Yoga is not against the law, and it is our backyard. There's a fence. She shouldn't be looking over it."

"I'd appreciate it if you kept your yoga clothed or at least in the house. That old lady is driving me crazy. Last week it was your music. The week before it was—"

"Yes, sir, we'll make sure we purport ourselves with a little more decorum in the future."

Sin tried not to snort. Saint might be innocent as could be, but the man could bullshit with the best of them.

"Ellison," Camden spoke.

With the authority in the Sheriff's voice, Sin couldn't mistake his twin's almost invisible shiver. Anyone else wouldn't have noticed, but he knew his brother and the man's fetish for dominating men. If only his twin would just give in and not let his shyness get in the way of them getting what they wanted.

"Sorry, we promise to try?"

"With the crews y'all hang out with that might be as good as I'm going to get."

"Would you like to have lunch with us, Sheriff?" Sin asked.

He batted his lashes and tried to move in close to Camden, but the man took a step back.

"No, I have work to do. You're not the only troublemakers I have in town. Behave."

It was the last thing Camden said before he left like his sexy, muscular ass was on fire.

"I swear that man fills out a pair of uniform pants like no other."

"He's going to arrest you for sexual harassment one of these days."

"As long as that man puts me in handcuffs, I don't care."

He smiled in victory as his twin giggled and closed his laptop.

"I'm serious, though. He's not interested."

"He so is."

"And what makes you say that? Every time he tells us no when we ask him on a date? Or when he turns on his toes and heads in the opposite direction when he sees us?"

It may seem weird to most people, but he wouldn't get into a serious relationship without his twin. They'd never spent a day or night away from each other in twenty-three years. They'd slept in the same bed their entire lives. They'd always known that whoever they ended up with would have to take them on as a package deal. Their mother raised them alone. She was everything to them, and never questioned or tried to discourage their loyalty between them. It would kill him to be away from his twin.

"He's an older man. We're a lot younger than him. It doesn't help we keep hitting on him."

"Hold up. You keep hitting on him."

"Semantics. If I'm hitting on him, it's us doing it. We're a package deal."

"But, Sin, I'm holding you back. Do you know how much easier your love life would be without you having to deal with my hang-ups?"

"I won't leave you. Men come and go, you're my twin, I loathe you some days—"

"Thanks."

"Shut up. You know what I mean. You want him. I want him, and that's the end. We'll get him. It's just going to take more finesse. Maybe you should take the lead on this one. You're a helluva lot less threatening than me."

"You definitely don't want him as much as I thought if you're trying to put me in charge. You're the confident one."

"Then we just have to change tactics."

"If you say so. Now, get back to work. If I don't have all the paperwork done for Fred tomorrow, he's going to get bitchy."

"Then back to work."

He smacked a kiss on his twin's cheek and went back to the stack of boxes he had to finish. Once he was hidden, he observed his brother. Saint was staring at the front door, his pointed chin rested on his palm, and Saint sighed heavily. The one and only experience Saint had, damaged him. He'd shown up in time before things went too far. He still remembered his brother telling the man to stop. If he hadn't come back from the store in time—he didn't want to imagine what could've happened.

He just wanted his brother happy. He was positive the Sheriff could do that. And it wasn't like he didn't want Camden too. He'd lusted after the man since he's spotted him the first time, so had Saint, but his brother was terrified of trusting someone. No matter what, he'd make sure it never happened again. He needed to get his twin and the sexy Sheriff on board with the plan. A relationship between the three of them was a done deal, Saint and Camden just didn't know it yet.

3 He Was Too Old for This Shit

Camden stared through the bars of one of the cells to watch one of his friend's mother glare right back at him. For all Mary Webb's innocent appearance, she spent a lot of time in that cell. He would've laughed at her cute little huff, and her arms crossed over her chest, but he knew the terror that existed in that sweet little brunette.

"Mary, we have to stop doing this."

Mary placed her tiny hands on the swell of her stomach. The woman kept a lot of distance between her stomach and people, except for her husband, Bear.

"I didn't do anything. The man tripped, and his face happened to connect with my fist."

He lost it then. He swore he didn't know how her new husband put up with her. Bear was a nice guy, and when you saw Mary and Bear together, it was rare not to see Bear having his tiny wife in his arms keeping her close. Marriage and love hadn't improved her temperament at all and Bear didn't mind in the least.

It's something he'd noticed about the couples there in Powers. Like his cousin, Scary, the man was a beast, the biggest asshole around, but when it came to Scary's husbands, Elijah and Tank, the man was a huge softie. It was odd. His friends, Psycho and Joker, were two of the most fearsome men in town and their husbands couldn't love them more. His jealousy was truly pathetic.

Everyone reminded him he was the target of Eric and Ellison. They were blond, blue-eyed and beautiful, almost ethereally so, especially Ellison. He was timid and appeared innocent while Eric was anything but. Ellison's submissive nature drew him, but Eric's bratty nature was an equal lure. He just didn't know if he could let his guard down. He'd kept his nature in check for decades while he built a career in law enforcement that he didn't really like. He surprisingly enjoyed his job as Sheriff. The place was low key, crime rate except for petty things was low, and most nights he got to sleep.

He pulled his dysfunctional brain away from the twins and back to his current repeat offender.

"Where's Bear?"

She jerked around to face him. "Why you want to know that?"

"Where's your husband?"

Mary tilted her chin up and tried to stand taller, then did this weird side-eye thing.

"He has nothing to see here, and you're going to let me out anyway."

"I am, but you get in more trouble when Bear's not cuddling you."

"He gives great cuddles."

Her cheeks turned pink when he unlocked the cell door, and she stepped out. She still kept plenty of space between them. The abuse Mary suffered at a young age caused her to shy away from everyone except her husband. She came around there a lot, though. He could almost say that they'd become friends even if he had to arrest her quite often.

"You need a ride home?"

"Nope, meeting Sin and Saint."

Before he could stop himself, he groaned at the mention of the Twin's names.

"You know those boys really like you."

"Too—"

"Fuck that too young shit. Sometimes you get one chance. Go for it. What's the worst thing that could happen? Temporary great sex…people should be so lucky to complain about that shit."

He didn't have a chance to say anything as she waved over her shoulder and disappeared up the steps, then he followed after her. She was already gone when he reached the main room. How she still moved that fast with her big stomach shocked him. He walked into his office and closed himself inside shutting the blinds.

He fell back into his desk chair and scrubbed his hands over his face. Even under his fingertips, he could tell the lines in his face were deeper; his goatee and mustache were longer than they should be. He felt older than his forty-five years. Abstinence wasn't a natural state for him, but he hadn't had a partner temporary or otherwise in almost five years.

In his previous line of work as an undercover agent, he hadn't had a guarantee he'd make it home from his assignments. He hadn't considered that fair to a partner. He'd seen too many significant others left behind. How could he with a good conscience do that to someone he'd claimed to love—he couldn't. So, he'd remained single, but having someone even temporary was painful. Forcing himself not to become attached—to develop feelings other than an urge to get off.

As Sheriff, he still worked under a cloud of danger but not as much as before. Part of him hadn't minded the years of being alone besides his team. That changed the day he'd met Eric and Ellison. He lusted, craved, and wanted to possess them. Although they were identical, it was easy to tell them apart.

Ellison had this innocence about him. Perfect creamy complexion with big, blue eyes and pouted pink lips. He carried a softness, slightly chunky and he wanted to find out what that softness felt like against him.

Eric was all slim angles and smart mouth, but with the same complexion, eyes, and lips like his brother. Eric was bratty, but he still possessed the same appearance of innocence as Ellison.

Neither made any secret they'd be a package deal. He couldn't have one without the other, and he wouldn't have thought about it anyway. The twins were close. They were rarely seen apart.

Did he want them? Yes. Would he do anything about it? He really didn't know.

Everyone gave him shit about it, but it was always done with a smile. No disgust or condescension. His cousin made it work with his two men. As far as he could tell, they were insanely happy. Then one of his deputies, Wren Gramble, was married to two men, Hunter and Linus.

It wasn't like he didn't have great examples of ménage relationships. Eric and Ellison were just so young. He wasn't—

A knock took him by surprise.

"Enter."

The door eased open, and he jumped to his feet when Ellison peeked inside.

"I'm...I'm not disturbing you...am I?"

He felt like an ass for his thought that Ellison's stutter was cute when he was nervous.

"Not at all, please, come in. Are you okay?"

Ellison's smiled shyly. "Yes. Mary said you were here alone and you hadn't eaten, I made extra and thought you might like it."

Ellison held out a small basket, but still just a step away from the door.

"You can come in." He took a seat hoping it would put the much smaller man at ease.

"Okay," Ellison said. Once inside Ellison got to work laying out a large checked napkin and setting the food on top of it. Sitting down, he was almost as tall as Ellison.

Ellison was all nervous energy and shooting him quick peeks, but pretending he wasn't.

"Are you going to join me?"

"No, no, this is all yours."

"You're going to sit down and share with me."

"Ye...yes, sir."

"Pull a chair around and sit beside me."

Ellison nodded and obeyed.

He divided the thick club sandwich, gave Ellison the chips, and stood to grab a few bottles of water from the small fridge in the corner of his office. When he returned to his desk, he handed one to the young man and took a seat. He observed the boy open the chips, then tore the side.

"Are Mary and Eric waiting for you?"

"No. Mary and Sin are doing some shopping, a present for Bear."

"I don't want to know."

He caught the small grin as Ellison tried to conceal it.

"You and Eric behaving?"

"Do you want me to lie?"

"So, you haven't—"

"No. Sin always gets in trouble. I prefer to stay to myself or take a trip in my plane."

He'd heard and witnessed Ellison's skill as a pilot. The boy was a bit of a daredevil as well.

"How did you become a pilot?"

"An old boyfriend of our mama was a pilot. He used to take us out and let me take over. I fell in love with the freedom."

"Your mother still alive?"

"Yes, she's on a year-long climbing and base-jumping trip. A lot of hiking and camping too."

"So you got it naturally."

"I guess so. Ernie still owns the old airfield out next to your place."

He nearly rolled his eyes. Ernie spent time in prison for smuggling drugs to Mexico, but as far as he knew, the man had turned his life around. That didn't mean he didn't keep a close eye on him since he owned the property next to Ernie's. He should've put two and two together, maybe living there was making him lose his edge.

"He's clean now."

"I'm sure he is."

"He is, he straightened up when he hooked up with Mama. She didn't put up with his shit. Told him if she caught him going back to his old life he was out."

"Why aren't they still together?"

24

"Oh, Mama gets bored easy. He stuck around for us, but they went their separate ways without hurt feelings. He liked being a dad so he kept us when we couldn't go with Mama."

"I was told you two tried modeling for a while."

Ellison stopped eating and worried the paper napkin between his fingers, tearing it to tiny pieces.

He took Ellison's hands in one of his. They shook under his larger hand, and he took in the contrast of light to dark.

"Talk."

"It was more Sin's thing. I was just along for the ride. They always said I was too fat."

"There's nothing fat about you, Ellison."

Long, pale lashes lifted and Ellison looked at him, there was a small, shy smile on Ellison's perfect mouth.

"Thank you."

Eric's confidence and attitude overshadowed Ellison's shyness and insecurity, obliterating it to the point that it may never have existed at all. That's when it hit him, Eric was Ellison's protector and mask. They were so similar that in casual passing you couldn't tell one from the other, but not him. He'd studied them both. Even when it appeared he was running—they always had his full attention.

"You're welcome. Now finish eating." He waited until Ellison started nibbling at the sandwich again. "I'm surprised Eric isn't with you, you two are pretty inseparable."

"We are, except when he has a date, but he always comes home."

He made a non-committal sound and forced down the last of his dinner.

He didn't like the sound of Eric dating. Or the nights he'd spent at Brawlers with a barely concealed fury as he watched someone else touch who he secretly considered his. It was an asshole attitude. He knew he couldn't have them, so he couldn't be angry when they found someone else. Ellison seemed to avoid the attention though. If Eric wasn't around, then Ellison used one of the crew as a shield.

He'd heard rumors about the siblings' unusual closeness. They constantly touched. When parted, they'd search each other out and wouldn't relax until they spotted their twin. It was joked about, but he didn't think it was too far from the truth that the two couldn't exist without the other.

"I should get back to work."

"I'll give you a ride."

"No, that's—"

"It's late, and I'm taking you."

"Yes, sir."

"Finish up while I check to make sure everything is locked up."

He stood and left the office.

One of the other deputies would check in later since they ran a pretty small crew around there. With a town like Powers, not a lot went down, and all the businesses have his cellphone number if they had trouble. Emergency calls were routed to dispatch at the fire department/EMS, then whoever was on duty was contacted. It had taken some getting used to and being on call twenty-four-seven wasn't new, but being the Sheriff, he was always on duty.

Wren covered if he needed time off, but it wasn't usually more than a weekend or a day here and there.

By the time he checked the building and returned to his office, Ellison had cleaned up and was waiting in the same spot he left Ellison. Ellison wore an oversized v-neck that exposed one freckled shoulder. He'd kept his libido in check, but that creamy skin drew him. He hadn't been able to ignore the sweet scent coming off the small man. The distance he'd kept between him and the twins was the only way to keep them safe from him.

He jerked off most nights to visions of his handprint on their pale skin, his teeth marks marking his territory. He wanted nothing more than to bend Ellison over his desk and fuck the slim body until his boy screamed his name. For years he'd kept his kink in check. The need to control and take care of his partner ate at him. He required submission. He denied himself to the point his sex life, when he had one, was satisfactory at best.

Ellison submissive nature called to him like nothing had before. Eric might be bratty and over-confident, but he sensed the same in Eric. He knew they'd be perfect.

"Are you ready?"

"Yes."

"Come on."

He stepped aside as Ellison surged from the chair and tried to hurry past him. He caught the back of Ellison's shirt. He wanted to taste the man's soft lips, but all he did was lean down to brush a kiss on the smoothness of Ellison's forehead.

"Thank you for dinner."

"It wasn't—"

"Thank you for dinner."

"You're welcome."

"That's better. Am I taking you home or back to the shop?"

"Home. Sin and Mary were just going to get a few things, and then he was going home."

"You'll wear my helmet."

He led Ellison from the building to his parking space out back. He wrapped Ellison in his leather jacket and secured the helmet. Once he was satisfied his—shit, not his—that Ellison was warm and safe for the ride, he mounted and waited for Ellison to climb on behind him. He tried not to tense when slender arms and legs wrapped around him. He really shouldn't enjoy the slight weight of Ellison behind him. Ellison held himself stiff, and that wouldn't do. So he brought his arm around to splay his hand on Ellison's ass and move him forward until there wasn't an inch of space between them. He couldn't be sure, but he swore Ellison let out a small squeak.

He smirked as he pulled off. For the first time in a long while, he enjoyed his ride, the roar of the engine, and Ellison plastered against him. He couldn't get used to it, but he could savor it while he had the opportunity.

4 Fuck, He Felt Good

Saint didn't want to get off the bike. Camden smelled like leather, sweat, and spicy cologne, but it could be the man's leather jacket that was wrapped tightly around him. He'd dreamed of being that close to Camden for almost three years since he'd seen him the first time. Camden had been dressed in tactical gear. Looking badass and sexy, commanding. He'd wanted to crawl into the man's lap and never get up.

When he'd mounted behind Camden, he'd tried to keep as much distance as possible between them, but Camden moved him closer. His brother saw something he wanted, and he went for it, except when it came to Camden. Sin was as terrified as him but played a good game. They'd never wanted the same person before. They always talked about it, and when it happened, he would be the one for them.

They hadn't anticipated, well, Sin hadn't anticipated their one putting up such a fight. He wasn't like Sin. He wasn't confident or outgoing. He wanted someone who would love and take care of him—someone to make decisions. Sin joked about his Daddy issues. He knew Sin didn't mean anything by it, but it hurt.

Camden had told him what to do—that he would eat. That he would sit beside him. He'd gotten hard at the commanding, gruff voice.

His chest hurt as Camden slowed to a stop. The man helped him off, and he stood beside the bike as Camden removed the helmet. He started to remove the jacket.

"No, keep it, I'll get it next time."

"Next time?"

"You stop by."

"Okay." He started to back away, but Camden's huge hand wrapped around the back of his neck.

He found himself plastered to Camden's side. He twisted his hands in Camden's uniform shirt. Tilting his chin, he waited for the kiss. He wanted those firm, full mouth on his. Calloused fingertips pinched his chin, and the hand on his neck kneaded the muscles.

Another kiss landed on his forehead like before they'd left. Camden pulled back, and he looked into the man's gorgeous green eyes. He was so close he could see the yellow flecks around the pupils.

"You're so beautiful."

Lips brushed his left cheek, then the right, and Camden moved lower until the man's mouth hovered over his.

"No—"

A hard tug at his hair stopped him.

"I said you're beautiful, Ellison."

"Thank you."

He lowered his gaze then jerked it back up when Camden retreated.

"I'll wait here until you're inside."

He turned away as tears started to fill his eyes. He wouldn't embarrass himself, or at least he hoped—there was a jerk to the back of the leather jacket. He turned to look over his shoulder.

"You and Eric come out to my place this weekend."

"What time?"

"Six for dinner."

A smile tugged at the corners of his mouth, "Okay."

"Go inside…it's getting chilly. You two behave."

He waited until he was released and tried not to run to the house to give Sin the news. Excitement made his hands shake as he tried to get the door open. He pivoted to wave at Camden, but when the man didn't leave, he rushed inside and only then heard Camden's bike rev and take off.

"I know I didn't see what I think I saw," Sin screeched and bounced on his toes.

"Dinner, Saturday at six."

"Yes," Sin shouted. "That's great, but what about the little cuddle session with our man."

"He just kissed my forehead."

"Start from the beginning. I want every detail."

Sin grabbed him, dragged him toward the kitchen, and shoved him into one of the kitchen chairs. His twin set them up with beers and took the seat at the end of the table beside him.

His brother stared at him. Sin's smile widened the more he related. Sin claimed to always know that Camden would be theirs, but he still wasn't so sure.

"You're still being pessimistic, I can sense it."

"He didn't really kiss me."

"Our man had his lips on you, touched you, and invited us to his place for dinner. This is fucking huge. Don't get all negative. We got a date, say it with me, we got a date with Camden Pelter, come on, say it."

"We got a date with Camden Pelter."

"Yes, we did. It's fucking amazing. We must celebrate."

"No, he told us to behave."

"One last free for all. What's the worst that could happen?"

Those were infamous last words. Sin jumped up and took off running for the living room. Seconds later, music blasted from the other room. Old Lady Bremenger was probably already on the phone to complain about the noise.

He leaned back in the chair and remembered the feel of Camden's lips on his forehead, his cheeks, and the texture of his calloused hands. He'd fantasized about being taken—owned by Camden. Most of them consisted of him kneeling beside Camden, his cheek rested on Camden's thick thigh, and being commanded by Camden. Only one other person knew about his needs—his twin—and shared them as well.

They'd picked the Dominant they wanted, but would Camden want to take care of them as they wanted him to?

He hugged himself and turned his head to bury his face in the leather. The weight of the jacket felt right and comforting. Thin arms suddenly wrapped around his neck from behind, and Sin buried his face against his neck.

"I won't let it happen again, Saint, I promise."

It was a promise Sin had made thousands of times over the years, sometimes daily. He still remembered the day, almost seven years ago. Sin had gone out to sneak them snacks. All he'd wanted was a candy bar. He'd had nothing but plain salads and water for weeks. He'd even lost a few pounds. When the door had opened, he thought it was Sin, but it was their agent. The man had walked into their room. He'd made a comment about the one room and bed being the only one used.

He started talking disgusting things about him and Sin. One second the man was yelling and the next the man was on him. He was small and didn't possess a lot of strength, but he'd fought long enough for Sin to get back. Nothing happened, his virginity was as intact today as that night.

"Camden wouldn't do that to me."

"No, he wouldn't. There's nothing wrong with us. You're my brother—my best friend since that egg split."

"But what if he thinks we're weird?"

He smiled as Sin snorted and hugged him tighter.

"You do remember our friends and family, right? Camden's been around long enough to know we ain't normal."

"True. He did tell us to be at his place Saturday."

"Told or asked."

"It was more like an order."

"Oh, how we love that in a man. Okay, big brother, time for your bath and did you eat?"

"Camden made me share his dinner with him."

"Good, now, bath. What are we going to watch tonight?"

"I want horror."

"One gory, sadistic movie coming up."

He let Sin help him from the chair and then his twin pushed him toward the stairs. He slowly ascended the staircase—the steps creaked under his feet. He removed the jacket as he entered their bedroom and laid the heavy leather on the end of the bed.

He wanted it to work out. He hadn't dared to dream of one date with Camden. Maybe they had a chance at more. He craved it more than anything. They had a date, and he'd have to be happy with that—for now.

5 Saint Was Going to Puke, He Knows It

They stood arms linked outside Camden's house. The place was huge, too big for one person, but it was out in the middle of nowhere. They knew Camden liked his privacy. He turned to glance at his brother to find Saint looking a little pale. Oh, shit, not good.

"Hey, it's fine, you look beautiful, big brother."

He tried to get Saint to wear something other than the man's favorite bulky sweater, but the stretched neckline exposed one pale shoulder. Saint had even put on a little extra makeup than he normally would.

He had to admit he was as nervous as Saint. They'd wanted this for so long, and they finally had the opportunity to have Camden.

They tipped their heads back as a helicopter flew over. Ernie, their stepfather, just purchased a few new planes. He tugged Saint forward, or his twin would try to sneak over to the property next door to see the new toys he'd get to play with soon.

When they reached the bottom step, the door opened, and they froze. Camden's large frame blocked out the lights from inside creating an aura around him. They'd seen him in a uniform and tactical gear, maybe a t-shirt and jeans, even in slacks and a dress shirt for King's wedding. But tonight Camden wore a white dress shirt with the sleeves rolled up to exposed veined forearms, and Camden's jeans were worn white in some spots. The man was twice their size and intimidating.

"Come on in."

He tugged Saint forward and ascended to the porch landing. Camden stepped aside, and they both entered. Dark hardwood floors gleamed under soft lamplight. A wide stairway led up to the second floor.

They'd been there a few times. Even got nosy and checked out every room in the place while Camden wasn't looking of course. He and Saint loved the house. The furniture was large and masculine, perfect for someone Camden's size. Art and pictures filled the walls. Bookcases were filled with more books than he'd seen in his life and what looked like family photos. Across the entryway was an office, and the sliding doors open exposing more book-lined shelves.

"Let me take your jackets."

Camden came up behind them, even standing a foot or more away, Sin swore he could feel the man's presence. He released Saint's hand. Camden removed Saint's jacket, then his, and moved away to hang them on a rack beside the front door.

"You two are awful quiet."

Saint fumbled for his hand again. He hated that his brother was so nervous. He'd tried his hardest over the years to work on Saint's confidence, but nothing he did seemed to put the man at ease for long.

"Ellison, look at me." Camden's voice was commanding.

Saint didn't hesitate to turn around, and it surprised him Saint gave in so quickly. He observed the way Camden raised his hand to stroke Saint's cheek and his brother leaned into the caress. They looked good together, the much larger man and his slim, short brother were the perfect contrast.

"What's wrong?"

"I'm nervous."

"Nothing to be nervous about. Just a meal. Is that okay?"

"Yes, sir."

He sensed when Saint calmed and it amazed him. He'd known from the moment he'd met Camden that the older man would be perfect for them, especially Saint. He wanted Camden just as much as Saint did, but in order for this to work between the three of them, Saint needed a certain level of dominance for his natural submissiveness. He pretended well, but Sin required the same.

"Good boy. I have to check on dinner, go on back to the kitchen."

They linked hands again and went in the direction Camden specified. He wondered what this was about. Why Camden suddenly invited them out to his place for dinner. The man had the perfect poker face and didn't give anything away.

They entered the kitchen to find the table set, a plate at the head of the table and one more on either side. He glanced at Saint, and they shared a smile at the candles flickering in the middle of the table. They'd never had a romantic candlelit dinner before and the fact that big and bad Camden Pelter prepared them one was odd, but nice.

"I don't drink at home so you two won't either. I have iced tea, water, and some sodas. What would you two like?"

It wasn't like they were going to fight Camden on the no drinking rule. They spent a lot of time at Brawlers and clubs, but they didn't drink more than a beer or two.

"Iced tea, please," they answered in unison.

"Take your seats."

They separated and sat at the table, then stared at each other across the expanse. He looked up as Camden set a perspiring glass next to the plate. His mouth dropped open as Camden leaned down and pressed a kiss to his forehead. Instant hard-on. How could someone make a forehead kiss erotic? He didn't know, but Camden sure as fuck did. He watched as Camden repeated the same with Saint.

Saint's long blond lashes fell and concealed his eyes. It was as if all the tension drained from his brother in a second. A small smile tilted the corners of his mouth as Saint opened his eyes, glancing up at Camden with the sweetest expression on his face. If nothing else had proved to him that Camden was theirs, then that moment would've sealed it.

Camden started moving around the kitchen, then serving bowls of roasted vegetables, mashed potatoes and gravy were placed on the table. A small roasting pan was the last and Camden sat down. Without asking, Camden fixed both their plates and made sure they had everything they needed before Camden filled his own.

The man was super sweet in Camden's own way, caring if a bit gruff. He sensed that Camden liked to be in control, take care of his partner or in their case, partners. Their mother and extended family weren't the religious sort, but they waited in case Camden wanted to do the whole Grace thing.

"Eat."

"We didn't know if you prayed."

"No."

They settled in to have dinner in silence. It was comfortable and nice. The food was amazing. Saint was the cook. He'd scorched a pan of water once, and Saint hadn't let him near the kitchen again. It surprised him a bit that Camden cooked, but it shouldn't have.

"Where did you learn to cook?"

"My maternal grandmother, she raised me."

"Oh."

"It's nothing deep and dark, Eric. My mother focused on her career to the detriment of everything else, and my father was the same. They hadn't grown up poor, middle class, but they saw their worth in having the nicest things they could brag about. I didn't live with my grandmother, but I spent a majority of my growing up with her. Ellison said your mother was away on a trip?"

"Yeah, she works as an adventure guide. Plans these elaborate trips, everything from mountain climbing to survivalist trips."

"Is there a reason she got into that?"

"Our dad. She met him when she wanted to learn to skydive during Spring Break. She got pregnant pretty quick, they didn't marry or anything, but they moved in together. Mama is always happy when she tells stories about him. He was climbing one day, and his rigging gave, he fell."

"I'm very sorry."

"Like Mama said, he died doing what he loved. Couldn't ask for more than that. They'd started the company, and Mama was great at it, so she continued it after he died. We think it was a way to keep his memory alive."

"Did you two work in the family business?"

"I worked as a guide in my teens. When Saint became interested in being a pilot, he started flying groups around. Piloting the jump planes."

"Did you enjoy that, Ellison?"

He liked that Camden didn't use their nicknames, even their mother had taken to calling them Sin and Saint. When Camden called them Eric and Ellison, it seemed special. It was also nice to see Saint included. His twin had a tendency to retreat and let him take care of conversation because Saint hated to be the center of attention.

"Very much, Ernie says I was a natural. Born to fly. He just bought a new Cessna and chopper."

"Was that him flying over when you two got here?"

"Yes, sir. He was testing them before I take them up this weekend."

"Maybe I should speak with him and make sure."

"Ernie wouldn't do anything to intentionally hurt us. He makes sure everything is in perfect condition before I even sit in the pilot seat."

"I'll speak with him anyway."

"Yes, sir." Saint lowered his chin.

He was about to say something when Camden placed his fingers beneath Saint's pointed chin.

"None of that. Now eat, you've been picking at your food."

"May I speak freely," he asked.

Camden turned to watch him with beautiful green eyes.

"Go ahead."

"What's going on here? You ordered us to dinner out of the blue when you've avoided us at all costs the last few years. Not that we're complaining, dinner with our favorite Law Enforcement Officer isn't a hardship. Are you not out?"

He peeked at his brother to find Saint watching Camden, too. He turned his attention back to Camden in time to catch the man's heavy sigh, and Camden set his fork on the edge of the plate.

"I'm not out, but I'm not in the closet either. My private life is just that, private. When I was offered the job as Sheriff, I took it because I needed a break. Having a personal life wasn't possible in my old job. Undercover work doesn't allow for healthy relationships when you have to be gone for months at a time sometimes, maybe with the occasional trip home. It didn't seem fair."

"So, you just got used to not saying anything?"

"Yes, but I wanted things to be different when I moved here. Twenty years of routine is hard to break."

"We're not exactly the secretive type. We've never been in the closet."

He hated the way his stomach dropped. Was this a *leave me alone* meal? They'd be crushed if Camden didn't want to have anything to do with them or keep their relationship on the down low. It wouldn't be fair to Saint. His brother deserved it all, from the public displays of affection to the chance of a ring on his finger one day.

"I wouldn't ask that of you or Ellison, that wouldn't be fair to either of you. I invited the two of you here to talk."

"So, you don't want to—"

He caught Saint nervously biting his bottom lip. He jerked his gaze to Camden as a chair slid across the floor.

"Ellison, come here."

If Saint didn't obey, he sure as hell would. Camden's voice commanded, and anyone would be helpless to say no. The man could read the goddamned bible and make it sound dirty.

"Ellison, I don't like to repeat myself."

Saint stood and took the few steps that separated them. Camden patted his right thigh, and Saint stepped around to stand between Camden's thighs before taking a seat. Camden lifted his hand to stroke Saint's cheek and tipped Saint's chin up until Camden and Saint's gazes met. Saint's pale cheeks were stained pink.

"Now, do you want to finish your question?"

"You don't want to date us. If you like Sin more, I don't mind."

He jerked like his brother had punched him. They'd discussed this so many times he'd lost count. It was an agreement they'd promised each other. They would find their man, and they'd be happy.

"Ellison, I don't like to be lied to. With that warning out of the way, why do you think I'd like Eric more?"

He held his breath waiting for his twin's answer. Saint dropped his gaze. Camden's large hand encompassed Saint's jaw and gently forced Saint to look at the bigger man.

The intensity in Camden's eyes was equal parts intimidating and caring. Camden cared what Saint's issue was, and he was helpless to look away from the two men.

"Ellison, if you're going to speak to me, you'll look me in the eyes."

"I'm not as skinny—"

"I'm going to stop you right there. I won't dismiss your insecurities because we all have them, but to me, you're beautiful, and a little extra weight doesn't and won't ever change that. Understood?"

"Yes, sir."

He held his breath as Camden straightened and leaned into Saint. The man's mouth barely an inch from Saint's. He wanted that kiss for his brother. His twin kept himself separated from everyone; there but not. Saint preferred his invisibility. It was time Saint's wishes came true.

"Ellison, how could you not know?" Camden asked the question, but the man didn't give Saint a chance to answer.

Camden and Saint's lips conformed to each others' perfectly. Saint made a tiny, needy sound and Camden growled. Camden curved his thick fingers around the back of Saint's neck.

Saint looped his thin arms around Camden and held their man tight. Camden's hand quickly wrapped around his wrist and pulled him onto the big man's free thigh. Camden nipped at Saint's lower lip and then turned his head toward him. Oh fuck, he'd imagined this so many times since they'd spotted Camden at Brawlers. But this, oh, this was so much better. Camden's lips were firm yet soft, conforming to his as easily as they had Saint's.

He moaned as Camden's tongue flicked over the seam of his mouth. He reached for Saint and held him close—he needed an anchor, and Saint was that for him. The kiss ended far too soon, but it was more than they'd expected. A few more soft, fleeting caresses and Camden helped them up, then back into their chairs.

Was that the kiss-off they feared or the start of something more? It couldn't be that easy. When he glanced at Saint, he saw his question and apprehension mirrored in identical eyes. He needed to be strong. Saint needed him to hold it together and like he'd done for twenty-three years, he might break, but Saint would always come out whole after the tears and a broken heart.

6 Shit, What the Fuck had He Done?

He'd kiss his boys goodbye last night beside their car after spending most of the evening with Eric and Ellison curled up on the couch on either side of him. Hours later, he swore he could still feel the softness of their lips and silkiness of their hair as he had run his fingers through it as they watched a movie. They're heads on his lap, and their delicate fingers twined together. The closeness of the twins was something he'd thought about but never really understood the true bond. They each sought comfort from the other and couldn't exist in the same space without touching.

Shit, what the fuck had he done? The dinner invite had been a spur of the moment thing. Ellison's slim form had been wrapped around him, and he hadn't wanted to let him go, but he wanted Eric with the same intensity. He scrubbed his hands over his face and blew out a heavy breath. The promise he'd made to himself after their first meeting was obliterated with one impulsive dinner invite.

Spending the evening making them dinner, caring for them, and holding them—no way he could he let it go.

Their ages were still an issue, he was old enough to be their father, and they had so much—

"Pelter! Did you just come to sit your oversized ass in my office or you got something to say?"

Fuck, he'd spaced out. He jerked his gaze to his pissed off cousin.

"My crew's on their best behavior so what the fuck?"

"How the fuck do you take care of two men?"

Scary appeared confused, and then a slow smug smile spread across his mouth.

"Well, you fucking came to me for advice on your boys? You gotta be desperate, man."

"Don't bust my balls, I know we ain't—"

"We're family whether I like it or not."

"Thanks, I'm feeling the love."

He and Scary were never close. His dad, Scary's uncle, was a bit of a dick, well, more than a dick. His parents were the type to think everyone was lesser than those who didn't have the best or strive to be the best. His aunt made the mistake of falling in love with someone who skipped out on being a parent. He and Scary hadn't hung out much other than spending time at their grandmother's house. Scary, or Brawler as he was known back then, had run with the rough crowd. And him, he'd gone into the military and joined the SWAT team. The irony of asking his ex-con cousin about how to handling dating his men wasn't lost on him.

"Get off that high horse of yours. We're on opposite sides of the law but I been straight for years, but you're the prodigal son, so to speak. So, what the fuck is up?"

"I invited Eric and Ellison to my place for dinner."

"Keep going, man."

"I didn't exactly think through the date. I mean, shit, what the hell am I going to do with two twenty-three-year olds?"

"Fuck them."

He wasn't even shocked that Scary said that with a straight face.

"That's not what I meant."

"So, you don't want to fuck them?"

"I didn't say that either. You got two damn men. Wren has two husbands. How the fuck do y'all do it? Setting aside the fact I'm old enough to be their father, how does all this shit work?"

"Lots of fucking compromises. No secrets. Elijah demands complete honesty."

"I get that part. But how do you spend time with them together and separately? I don't know what the fuck I'm doing here."

"Rule one...honesty. The equal time thing, it's not always going to be perfect, but to be honest, all this shit is different. This ain't paint by numbers, man. This is where the honesty comes into play. You freaking out about the prospect of dating two men?"

"More their ages than the two."

"Stop right fucking there. Listen, if you're going to go all fucking noble and shit, you should walk away now."

"I don't think I can."

"Then do this, sit down and discuss your expectations and theirs. Sin and Saint are almost creepily close, but that might just be that twin shit."

The office door flew open behind him, and as he reached for his service weapon, Scary reached under his desk.

"What the fuck, Linus? Didn't you learn from the last time you pulled that shit?"

Linus grinned, and it was too much like his brother Lucky's mischievous expression, and it meant trouble.

"Nice patch job by the way and you missed by a fucking mile last time."

"What the hell do you want?"

"Um, you and Pelter in the same room for an extended period. Battle of the Beasts, man, we've got money on this shit, and I'm here to witness."

As an atheist, he didn't think there would ever be a situation where he'd believe in Hell, but this was it. He was in Hell. Linus was too nosy for his own damn good.

"How the hell did you even know I was here?"

"Wren called said you were off to Brawlers, Bear and Ben called said you'd just drove passed their shops. Then a group message was started, and the bets were coming in. I was the only one crazy enough to witness, oh, Lucky or Psycho would've come, but they had kid duty."

"We're not going to fight."

"Then what the hell are you doing here, we got trouble?" All the amusement disappeared from Linus' expression, and he was all business.

It wasn't about trouble, but he felt there was some brewing. He just needed more information before he asked Linus and the Trenton Crew for help. He had more pressing issues to take care of, and that was making sure he did right by Ellison and Eric.

"No, I wanted to ask Scary something. I think I'm going to go. This was a—"

"Is this about getting the twins on your dick?" Linus asked with a straight face. "Oh, man, that's the newest gossip, heard you had them out at your place."

Linus strode across the office and perched on the corner of Scary's desk.

He surged to his feet and clenched his fists. "Is my sex life a bet too?"

"Naw, man, we figured you'd give in sooner or later. What the fuck is the problem?"

He darted a glance from Linus to Scary, he didn't want to go back to the play by play of being too old or them too young, or the one thing he hadn't told them—he was fucking terrified.

"He doesn't know what to do with two of them," Scary answered for him.

"Fuck them."

"What the fuck is it with you two? Fuck them isn't an answer. Not that I don't want to, because I do, but how the hell do I keep two of them happy?"

"Is that what this is about? You ain't the first man in history having to keep two partners happy. But you don't gotta hide them from each other, bonus."

It was well-known Linus had avoided commitment before Wren and Hunter came along and that he'd had plenty of open relationships. For as long as he'd known Linus the man was seeing at least two people, male and female. He didn't get it, he liked monogamy, and one day hoped he'd have someone to come home to, but this situation hadn't ever even been a blip in his thoughts.

"What about the twenty-two-year age difference?"

"Minor issue and you know you want those boys to call you Daddy so bad you're about to nut in your pants."

"What the fuck are you talking about?" He jerked his gaze to Scary to find the man all smug.

"Oh, come on, this is just us, admit it, you want to take care of those two boys. You want them happy and content. Don't think I didn't notice the way you watched them. You're protective as fuck and for an even-tempered man you get pretty pissed when someone even glanced at your boys. Do you remember the night King and Linc got married?"

"What about it?"

"You were hovering near them all night. They didn't notice, but we did. You sent plates of food. Made sure someone always refilled their drinks. Oh, and when they fell asleep that night, when you thought no one was around, you leaned down and kissed their foreheads and tucked their blankets around them. You're so a Daddy." Scary arched a brow and relaxed back in his desk chair.

Shit, he'd thought he'd been so careful that night. The temptation of them in his house. The urge to pick them up and carry them upstairs to his bed had overwhelmed him, yet he'd settled for just tucking them in. That night proved to him he needed to stay away from them.

"Don't panic." Linus held up his hands. "They didn't notice. Listen, me and Scary ain't exactly the people to come to for advice about your sex life or lack thereof, but what the fuck could it hurt? I mean, if those boys of yours aren't in love with you already, it's fucking close, and you can't tell me you don't feel the same."

He fell back into the chair he'd vacated and observed as Scary pulled a bottle of Top Shelf whiskey from his desk drawer.

"What if I'm not enough?"

"Never know unless you try, Camden. From what I remember when we were kids, you were a stubborn shit. You won't fuck this up, but if you don't stop keeping those boys at arm's length or sending them mixed signals, then you'll definitely fuck it up. Let's have a drink."

"I'm on—"

"Our last Sheriff was dealing drugs and people, you having one drink won't make no difference."

"Wren, baby, I got a favor—"

He turned to find Linus on his phone.

"Cover for Pelter. He's got an emergency to take care of..." Linus snorted. "Yeah, that kind of emergency. I'll make it up to you tonight, I promise."

Linus' smile when he talked to his men, or the way he relaxed when they were around, was as far removed from the man he knew that it could get. Linus was hard and a bit cold, but for Hunter and Wren, the man was downright soft.

He nodded at Scary, and the man poured three doubles. He hadn't known what to expect when he came to Scary for advice, but part of him prepared for more snark and insults. He and his cousin were never close. He was closer to Linus even though he threatened to bust him and his crew hundreds of times over the years.

Everything had changed so much since he'd moved there and taken over the job as Sheriff. But he wouldn't change it for the world. He finally found somewhere he belonged. He just needed to figure out how to make his two men happy.

7 They're Going to Need Bail Money

"Pass it, pass it." Lucky had his arm in the air, and it took several tries for Saint to pass the joint. Naked Stoner Saturday Night was in full swing. Sin was laying with his head on his stomach, and Twitch was sprawled sideways on top of Lucky's midsection. Twitch had a massive crazy straw in a coffee milkshake. Eli was stoned as fuck, and he didn't even want to know what that man was texting his men all night. He may have heard camera clicks a few times.

Priest was seated on the couch smiling indulgently at them all cuddle-piled on the floor of Lucky and Priest's living room. Priest was always their designated munchies runner.

Normally most of the partners showed up to hang out while the big guys took care of the kids, but a cold took down most of the mini-humans. Lily and Damon had taken Matty for the night.

"I have a question." Twitch flopped over on Lucky's stomach, and Lucky grunted. "Pelter, are we talking—" Twitch held his hands a few inches apart. "Or are we talking?" Twitch held his arms as wide as they would go.

"Now, Twitch—" Lucky stroked Twitch's hair. "If he were—" Lucky mimicked Twitch. "That would be nothing but the tip and really what fun is just the fucking tip?"

Saint raised his hand to hide his face that he knew was on fire, then dropped his hand as Sin giggled.

"But, but, have you seen our man in his uniform pants, he's definitely not…" Sin held his hand inches apart. "And we got lap time, man, lap time. His thighs are amazing." Sin turned amazing into twenty syllables with an obscene moan.

"Lap time? Why are we just hearing? I love Crave lap time."

"Twitch, baby, if you two wouldn't get arrested, Crave would have you on his dick twenty-four-seven." Lucky tugged gently on Twitch's long dark hair and he grinned at his friends.

"It is nice when he—"

"Do I really need to be hearing this?" Elijah groaned.

"Oh, don't even start. I've walked into the office to find your men in the same…oh my fake baby Jesus, Elijah, how do they fit? You must spend a ton on lube. How do you walk?"

He laughed at Twitch's wide-eyed stare and then Twitch was sucking on his straw again.

The joint made two more rounds in silence. Then he felt like he couldn't move. No cares in the world, just relaxed, and his usual anxiety was nowhere in sight.

"So, y'all gonna spill or what? We're old married men, boring." Lucky laid his arm to the side and played with his hair.

Lucky knew he found comfort in having his head rubbed.

Priest huffed from the couch. "You want boring? I'll put your hippie ass on the couch."

"Baby…" Lucky rolled dropping Twitch to the carpet with a grunt and Lucky crawled to Priest. He smiled at the two men. He waited for embarrassment, even though most of them didn't have issues with being nude around each other. He'd found some comfort since hanging out with the partners. They were supportive and protective, and there wasn't any doubt they all loved each other like family.

Priest's book was removed, and then Lucky was between his husband's spread legs. The kiss was almost obscene, but he was jealous too. The relationships all his friends had were envy-inducing.

"You know I love you, more today than the day I got my ring on your finger. You're my everything."

He stroked his fingers through Sin's hair. He chuckled as Twitch let out a heavy sigh with his cute chin cupped in his palms. Lucky turned around and sat at Priest's feet, Priest twisting Lucky's locs up.

"Share with the fucking class. Y'all have been waiting for this shit."

"He had us out for dinner."

"And? I'm not pulling teeth to get answers." Lucky leaned forward and tugged at his hair.

"Why aren't you asking Sin?"

Elijah's soft hair stroked along his cheek then the man's head was rested on his shoulder, their cheeks pressed together.

"Because we know how Sin feels about it, but we know you're not all in."

"I am, Eli, I promise, I just…Camden can have anyone and Sin is—"

"Don't start that shit again. I'd felt like you'd slapped me when you told Camden if he preferred me. That hurt, Saint."

"I'm sorry."

"Don't be sorry, just fix your shit."

"I want ice cream, munchies run!" Twitch jumped up and ran toward the bedroom.

"Why the fuck is he always the first one to get the munchies?"

"Because that boy has zero body fat." Sin rolled to his feet. He giggled a bit when he stumbled as he straightened.

"You're talking about someone having zero body fat."

"Look at this!" Sin could barely get his fingers around the skin on his belly.

"Everyone get dressed. If we're making a run, let's do it now," Priest ordered as he grabbed Lucky's hands in his and pulled the man to his feet.

The look of joy on Lucky and Priest's faces were enough to make a person sigh. The two men headed for their bedroom, and he nearly jumped when Sin's arm went around his waist.

"I want that."

"Big brother, we'll have it. Camden is it for us, remember?"

"What if he doesn't want to be ours?"

"He does, the kiss proved it to me. We just have to be patient, but now I want ice cream."

He laughed as Sin dragged him off to the guest room where they found Twitch dragging on his skinny jeans and trying to stay on his feet.

"You hold him, and I'll pull his pants up."

"Yeah, we're never going to get our ice cream if we don't."

Thirty minutes later after stuffing a giggling and wriggling Twitch into his clothes and driving to Granger Grocery, they sat outside with pints of ice cream and plastic spoons.

"Oh fake baby Jesus, this is soooo good." Twitch's moan was vulgar.

"You know what would make ice cream better?" Lucky asked.

"What?" they all asked.

"After sex ice cream or during, chest and pubes sticky, licking—"

The statement ended on muffled words as Priest slammed his hand over his husband's mouth. They all giggled at Priest's red-stained face.

"Crave likes licking ice cream off my—"

He muffled Twitch's statement and earned himself a lick.

"That's so gross. I know where your mouth has been."

He scrubbed his wet, sticky palm on his jeans and went back to his ice cream. It was after seven, so the streets had cleared out a bit, but some people still littered the sidewalks, coming and going from the businesses that were off the main drag.

He still had that heavy, relaxed feeling from smoking earlier, but it was slowly ebbing away. He'd relived the kiss Camden gave him so many times in the past week. He loved the gentleness of it and the way Camden made him feel like he was the center of his attention even when Camden turned to give Sin a kiss. Camden had still held him tight and stroked his back.

"Is there a reason y'all are loitering outside the grocery store?" Camden's big, booming voice was deep with authority.

He jerked his head up to find Scary, Linus and Crave standing behind Camden.

"Baby, aren't y'all supposed to be out at Lucky's place?" Crave asked as he stepped forward and crouched in front of Twitch.

"Munchies," Twitch said as if that explained everything then spooned ice cream passed Crave's smile.

"Mocha Java ice cream, what is the rule?"

"But it's so good."

"Want to take that ice cream home?"

Twitch bounced. "Can we?"

"Yes, we can."

He couldn't help smiling as Crave scooped Twitch into his arms. "I'm going to have to skip dinner. I just got other plans."

"Told you so," Twitch sang as he was carried off toward Crave's bike.

"Elijah, you're awful quiet." Scary's voice was low as the big man mimicked Crave's actions.

"We need to buy all the ice cream. All. Of. It."

"Want to go home to our bed?"

"Is Tank home, because I really need—"

"You'll get the pounding you crave, I promise."

The normally chill Elijah was on his feet and headed for Scary's bike.

"I guess my man is ready. Pelter, come out next weekend for a run, plan it or we'll come get your ass."

That was all Scary said before he also left.

"Okay, since everyone else is getting laid, I'm going home to my men."

"We're going home if everyone is okay," Priest announced, but didn't wait for an answer.

They were quickly left alone with Camden still in the same spot beside his SUV. He couldn't read anything in Camden's expression. Sin had linked his arm through his, and their ice cream was forgotten. He sensed his nervousness mirrored that of his twin.

"Are you two hungry?" The tilt of Camden's full lips showed the big man knew it was a stupid question. "Come on. We'll go to the diner, and then I'll take you home." Camden closed the distance between them and held out his hands.

He didn't know why he felt the need to apologize, but he did. "Sorry, we ruined your man time."

He and Sin threw away the almost empty cartons of melted ice cream in a trash can in front of the store.

"Ellison, it's fine. I heard all the partners had a monthly sleepover thing."

Camden separated them and took their hands, strolling down the street toward the diner. At that time of night, it typically wasn't busy.

"Not as many as usual, most of the kids are down with colds. It was just the five of us tonight," Sin spoke.

He resisted the urge to look around Camden to his twin. Then he realized Camden was walking hand in hand with both of them, just like Elijah did with Scary and Tank. He wondered if the man knew what he was doing. That wasn't like keeping what he hoped was a relationship behind closed doors.

"Linus said Craig was sick and Hunter took the night off to stay home with him. Juvie is off taking care of Princess, Brody and Trouble took off for a week convention thing to represent Twirled."

"The kids spend so much time together they usually all get sick."

Camden released their hands and opened the diner door, instantly he and Sin reached for each other. He darted a look at Camden, but Camden acted like it was normal. He knew most people looked at them speculating and judging. It was what set their agent off the night the man attacked him.

"Ellison?" A rough palm stroked his cheek. "Are you okay?"

"Yes, sorry."

"Let's get some food in you two."

Camden led them to a booth in the far-right corner. He watched Camden nudge Sin in and then when the big man slid in…he dragged him in beside Camden.

"Well, this is new." Heidi owner and ever-present server stopped in front of the table. "Finally got your head out of your ass, Sheriff?"

"Why did I ever think moving to this town would be relaxing?"

"Because you're an idiot."

"I love you too, Heidi."

"I'm sure you do, but I don't have any of your favorite pie tonight."

"Get my boys orders, while I decide what I want since you don't have any pie. Ellison, Eric, order dinner."

He shyly studied the menu that hadn't changed in years and waited for Sin to order, and like always they'd decided on the same thing.

"I don't even have to ask, Saint."

He giggled as she jotted on her pad.

"Damn, Sheriff, I can feel my gray hairs multiplying waiting on you."

"How the hell do you keep business with this stellar customer service of yours?"

"I make great pie."

"Tease," Camden grumbled and ordered the biggest burger Heidi had on the menu with a double order of fries and coffee.

"At your age, Sheriff, do you think you need coffee this late."

Heidi lifted her perfectly waxed brow and looked at him and Sin, then back at Camden.

"Kiss my ass, Heidi."

Heidi snorted and walked away from the table.

"Come here often?" Sin asked.

"Cooking for one sucks and it's easier just to order something. Were y'all having fun tonight?"

"Do we need bail money or are you about to read us our Miranda rights?"

He tried to keep a straight face as Sin batted his lashes and attempted to look innocent. Camden groaned and scrubbed his hands over his face.

"Did I arrest any of you at King's wedding? I saw nothing."

"Kind of a weird attitude for a hard-assed Sheriff who's been strictly by the book since he took over."

"I don't have enough room for all of you in lockup. Tangling with the Crews would just be a pain in my ass. I'm not inviting trouble. I've seen Peaches in action. I'd never win."

Camden wrapped his big hand around his opposite knee and mirrored the same action with Saint. His anxiety eased away knowing Camden wasn't hiding them or public displays of affection. Maybe it would all work out, and he and Sin could have want they'd wanted for almost two years. Camden was theirs. He laid his cheek on Camden's thick bicep, and he instantly felt a kiss pressed to the top of his head.

All three of them sat there in silence until Heidi brought their food and they spoke very little over dinner, but it was a comfortable silence. One that he and Sin could exist in for hours because they knew each other so well. It was perfect, and he hoped it never ended.

8 This Wasn't Home, at Least Not Theirs

Sin watched the darkened scenery fly by outside the back window of Camden's big black SUV. When they'd left Heidi's, Pelter walked them back to his vehicle, and they'd headed in the opposite direction of his and Saint's place. He turned to study Camden, the man's face was illuminated by the dashboard lights. The big man was someone who commanded the space he was in, and no one could deny the dominance and power that rolled off Camden in waves.

He scooted to the middle of the seat and leaned forward to peek at Saint. He smiled finding his twin asleep.

"Why don't you have your seatbelt on?"

"And why are you not taking us home?"

"I said I was taking you home...I just didn't specify whose home."

"What changed your mind?" he whispered not wanting to wake Saint.

"My mother."

"You told your mother about us?"

"No. She called and ordered me to come for Christmas because I spent the last one with Scary. Two years in a row wouldn't be acceptable."

"And?"

"I asked if I could bring a date. She asked would the date be female. I came out decades ago a few days before I enlisted in the Marines. She knows damn well I wouldn't bring a woman. She wouldn't extend an invite if it wasn't a she I was inviting instead of a he. I came here, took this job wanting a different life for myself."

"Where you didn't hide?" He couldn't imagine hiding in a closet most of his life. His friends had shared the stories of the lack of acceptance from family and former friends. Their mama never mentioned their sexuality or who they chose to love at any point. She'd introduced her friends and colleagues' partners without hesitation, as if the gender of said partner didn't matter. So when they mentioned the boys they'd had crushes on, it was met with only a smile.

"That and with my previous job I couldn't subject someone to a visit to say I wasn't coming home. Not that this job has less danger, because even a town this quiet there's potential, but for the most part everyone is accepting."

"You know a lot of people in law enforcement and military have partners. You gotta think about it, is finding love and savoring the time you have better than not experiencing it at all?"

"Pretty wise."

"I may be twenty-three, but Saint and me are pretty grown up. We had a lot of freedom growing up. Our mama's job isn't the safest one out there. It just takes one flaw in a carabiner or rope, and your adrenaline high ends with a deadly fall. Mama lost Dad that way, but she cherished the short time she had with him. To her, it was worth it. Don't you think whoever you found would think you were worth it too?"

"I'm not the easiest man to get along with."

"Did we forget that Scary got two men, or Lucky and Priest? What about Crave and Twitch, or Bull and Gregory, Psycho and—"

Camden chuckled. "I get it."

He loved the lighter Camden. The one not being hard-assed all the time. He loved the Camden giving them a chance. He'd tried to stay positive for Saint, but he couldn't deny a part of him felt they'd never get Camden's agreement to be theirs.

"What are we going to do when we get to your house?"

"I want you two in my bed."

"And what would being in your bed entail, Sheriff?"

"For tonight, just sleep. Soon though, I won't be content with just sleeping between you two."

His cock hardened, and he shifted on the seat. He and Saint had envisioned what Camden would do to them so many times since they'd seen him. What it would be like to be fucked or made love to by the big man. He'd never slept beside anyone but Saint. Wouldn't everyone be surprised to know the most action he'd gotten in his twenty-three years was from his toys? He'd stupidly fucked one guy in his life, and that was the worst experience he'd ever had.

"Can I tell you a secret? Even Saint doesn't know."

"You can tell me anything, but can I ask why Ellison doesn't know?"

"I'm a little embarrassed."

"Then it will be just between the two of us until you're ready to share with him."

"All those nights Saint thought I was out getting laid. I wasn't. I slept with a guy once, and it hurt too much to enjoy."

"Didn't he take the time to love on you first?"

"I don't think he cared whether I liked it or not."

"Well, that won't happen with me."

"I didn't think it would," he said as they pulled off the main road onto the gravel drive to Camden's house. Quickly the big house came into view. "I always, no, Saint and me, fell in love with your house the first time we stepped inside."

"It was an impulse buy."

"Wow, my impulse buys are whether I want the name brand ice cream or the store brand."

Camden pulled to a stop in front of the white picket fence.

"I'd looked at renting one of the apartments over the businesses on Main Street, but the minute I saw this place, I had to have it. The listing was a year old, and the Realtor said that the owner didn't want to break up the land into smaller plots."

Camden turned off the vehicle, flipped through the keys and handed him the house key.

"Unlock the door, and I'll carry Ellison inside."

He opened the door and hopped out to run for the door. He glanced back over his shoulder and grinned at Camden with Saint gently cradled in his arms. No matter how many times he saw them together, he couldn't get over how great they looked together.

He reached inside and turned on the light, then stepped back to let Camden pass. He closed and locked the door behind them. A lamp was on in the living room, but he followed Camden up the steps to the second floor. All the doors were closed as they walked down the hall toward an opened doorway. His stomach started to knot the closer they approached Camden's bedroom.

Camden said nothing was going happen tonight, but it was the fact they'd be sleeping in bed with him that was nerve-wracking.

"Turn the bed down."

He rushed forward. The bed was huge compared to his and Saint's full-sized bed. He pulled the comforter and sheet down; then he stepped back to watch Camden slowly strip Saint of his shoes and clothes down to Saint's pink briefs.

"You're good with him."

Camden didn't reply until the big man had covered Saint and tucked him in tight. Camden straightened and turned to him.

"Am I good to you?" Camden asked.

The big man closed the distance between them, and he didn't know why, but he started backing up until the wall beside the door stopped him. Camden placed his hands flat beside his head.

"You going to answer me?"

A sexy smirk tilted one corner of Camden's full lips, and he swore he was going to melt right into the surface behind him.

"Do I make you nervous, Eric?"

He quickly nodded. He shouldn't be nervous. This is what he'd wanted for so long. He held his breath as Camden seemed to lower his mouth to his in slow motion. The feather-light kiss that landed on the corner of his mouth, then repeated on the other side surprising him.

He'd expected an all-out assault—something harder—but it was tender and slow. A seduction, that's what the kiss felt like.

He raised his arm to wrap around Camden's neck and then Camden's hands were on his waist lifting him up. Camden pinned him to the wall with his hips. He locked his ankles at the small of Camden's back. The big man let out a deep, rumbling growl and his dick hardened.

"Fuck, you're sexy. Do you know how hard it was to tell you two no that night at Brawlers?"

Camden brushed caresses to his mouth, the man's long goatee and mustache teasing his skin, and he swore his brain was shutting down.

"You wanted us then?"

Camden's hands bracketed his face, and rough thumbs stroked along the curve of his lower lip. The thick ridge of Camden's dick pushed to his ass, and he tried not to giggle as Twitch's question came to mind. That wouldn't come across as adult at all.

"You don't know how much. Part of me was pissed you came up to some random man in the bar, and the other wanted to take you both home with me."

"We would've gone."

Camden rested his forehead against his and sighed. "I know, baby, but I'm old."

"You're not old. Bull and Gregory…"

"I know, same age difference. I have tomorrow off, can you and Ellison spend it with me?"

"You're in luck, Fred works tomorrow."

"Good, I was going to tell you two to call in sick."

He chuckled as Camden lowered him to his feet. "We so would have."

"I'm going to jump in the shower."

"Want some company?"

"Get your ass in the bathroom."

His eyes went wide because he hadn't expected Camden to take him up on the offer. The sharp smack to his ass had him running to the bathroom off of Camden's bedroom. He turned to walk backward watching as Camden strode toward him. The big man pulled the hem of his uniform shirt from his jeans. Camden unbuttoned it exposing a thin line from his outie bellybutton to disappear into Camden's pants. Next was perfect abs and a powerful chest covered in tight black curls as Camden dragged it off his broad shoulders. No matter how many times he'd dreamed of this moment, nothing came close to reality.

He visually traced Camden's ink that covered both of the big man's ribs and both arms from shoulder to wrist. It was a mosaic of skulls, black roses, and Gothic scrollwork.

"Eric?"

He hadn't realized how distracted he'd become with looking at Camden. "Yes?"

"Strip."

Before the order completely left Camden's mouth, he reached behind and grabbed the back of his shirt. He dragged it over his head and let it fall to the floor. He swallowed hard as he undid his jeans and pushed them along with his underwear down his legs. When he kicked them aside, he stood there, his body shaking as Camden stared at him. Camden's eyes were heavy-lidded and dark as the man's gaze moved over him.

"More beautiful than I ever imagined."

Camden said it so quietly that he wondered if the man even knew he'd said it aloud. He watched as Camden bent at the waist, lifted his pant legs, and untied his black boots.

With efficient movements, Camden stripped, and his clothes made it to the pile.

Unholy fucking shit! He jerked terrified he'd said it out loud.

Camden was long, thick, and slightly curved to the left. Camden was hard, and the dark, fat head was glistening with pre-come. What shocked him more than the size was the Jacob's ladder of several small barbells that ran the length. He hadn't expected piercings.

Camden closed the few feet between them. He shuddered as Camden's hot skin met his for the first time. The tip of his cock bumped Camden's heavy balls as Camden's length pushed into his stomach. Camden's arm went around him, and he let Camden walk him backward.

He hugged Camden's waist as the man turned on the shower. The silence made him nervous. He tried to figure out what was going on in Camden's head. He sighed as he stepped under the hot spray, then hissed as his back was pushed to cold tile.

The water was suddenly turned off. Camden dropped to his knees, and the man's mouth latched onto his right nipple and bit. The pain, but strange pleasure, made him tip his head back. Then the suction was hard enough he knew Camden was leaving a mark. He curled his hands around the back of Camden's head, the stubble rough under his fingers and palms. Camden moved over his torso leaving sharp bites and stinging sucks. He moaned and tried to keep his thighs from shaking, but one second he was partially holding it together and then Camden swallowed the entire length of his dick.

He cried out at the extreme ecstasy. Camden growled and bobbed along his cock. He dropped his gaze to watch Camden sucking him off. The shock of the big man on his knees for him took his breath. He sucked in his stomach and curled forward—the pressure was too much. As a blunt finger pushed at his hole, he tensed and came embarrassingly quickly as the tip of Camden's finger pushed inside him.

He leaned boneless against the wall and then Camden's mouth was on his. The kiss wasn't like the one in the bedroom. This was a claiming. He tasted himself on Camden's tongue. The quickness of Camden spinning him and his cheek pressed against the tile shocked him.

"Camden—"

"Shh, baby, I'm not taking you tonight," Camden whispered in his ear as the man's huge hand splayed across his stomach. "But I need to come, and I want it on that sexy ass of yours." Camden flexed and bent him over slightly, and he flattened his hands against the wall.

Camden's dick notched between his cheeks, and the barbells felt odd in his crease. He imagined Camden's cock inside him, but he wasn't ready. Soon, but not yet. Camden's teeth sank into his shoulder as rode his crease. The man's heavy balls slapped against his thighs, and the jewelry rubbed his sensitive hole. Camden held tight to the front of his thighs—fingers digging in almost painful where leg met groin.

His man grunted while thrusting—the sounds and feel of Camden overwhelmed him. He'd just come, but his cock ached.

"You feel so fucking right. Perfect."

"Camden."

"No, baby, you know what I want to hear. Fucking say it, tell me."

He laid his forehead against the cool tile. The word repeated in his head. He'd known, they'd both sensed it, and he needed to give Camden what he wanted, what they all wanted. "Daddy."

"Fuck, boy, say it again. What do you want your Daddy to do?"

"Come on my ass, Daddy, please."

Camden's hand curved around the front of his throat and pulled his body into an arch. He felt Camden move away enough to stroke his cock, the head just pushing at his hole. The burn was slight, and then Camden arched behind him. The warmth of Camden's release painted his hole, and Camden's fingers contracted to tip his head back enough for Camden to kiss him as Camden continued to stroke, was amazing.

"Fuck." Camden hugged him back against him.

He felt safe and loved as Camden dropped kisses on his cheek and shoulder.

"You okay, baby? I didn't mean to let it go that far. I just wanted you to feel good."

"Perfect."

"Let's get cleaned up and then we'll go get into bed with Ellison."

He nodded, the water was turned back on, and Camden slowly and lovingly washed him from head to toe. He was turned on and hard again before Camden was done. Camden sat him on the tiled bench of the huge shower stall. He couldn't help the silly grin that he felt pulling at his mouth as he observed Camden take his own shower. He hadn't lied when he said this was perfect. Camden erased every bad memory he had.

Shortly, Camden had them both dried off and tucked into bed, him on one side of Camden and Saint on the other. Camden's arms around them both, their heads on his chest. His and Saint's dreams were coming true.

Camden brushed a kiss to both their foreheads before he closed his eyes, his mind quickly shutting down and he laced his fingers through Saint's as he fell asleep.

9 His Boys Were in His House Where They Belonged

Camden awoke to the oddness of someone else in the bed with him. He'd never slept with someone before especially not two someones. Eric and Ellison's smooth warm skin plastered to his sides and their slim legs thrown over his thighs. He smiled at their fingers still linked together. He'd watched them long after they fell asleep. A long time had passed since he'd opened his eyes not dreading his day. Normally he was up and already out the door, but he was content to lay there.

His boys groaned in unison, curled up until they were tucked under his arms.

"There better be coffee," Eric growled.

Wasn't that fucking cute? It would figure at least one of them wasn't a morning person.

"No, there isn't."

"That must be remedied." Sin lifted his head, gave him a quick kiss and rolled from the bed.

He didn't mention Sin's nakedness as the man left the room. No one ever came out there. He eased away from Ellison and tucked the covers back around him. The man was truly beautiful. He tucked Ellison's soft hair behind his ear and leaned forward to brush a kiss on Ellison's forehead. He got out of bed and headed to his bathroom to take a piss and brush his teeth.

He quickly took care of his morning routine, but instead of heading downstairs, he returned to bed. Ellison was on his back, his arms and legs sprawled across the bed. The scent of coffee traveled from the kitchen. Scary and Linus said splitting his time between the two wouldn't be perfect. He and Eric had spent time together. Yet now it was time for Ellison to have his undivided attention.

He lay back down, fisted his left hand in the covers and tugged the comforter and sheet down exposing Ellison's creamy skin. Freckles dotted his shoulders and chest. The little paunch of Ellison's stomach teased him, and he lay down kissing the softness. Ellison smelled like vanilla. He sucked and kissed from Ellison's belly upward. Ellison moaned and arched in his sleep. His dick hardened where it pressed against Ellison's thigh. He hugged his boy close as he gently kissed Ellison awake.

Slim arms twined around his neck, and Ellison lifted into his kiss.

Ellison lowered his head back to the pillow and gave him a sleepy smile.

"There better be coffee."

"Do you and Eric share a brain?"

"Is he making coffee?"

"Yes, he is." He stroked his hand down Ellison's chest enjoying the sight of his big, rough hand on Ellison's soft, flawless skin.

"He's always been my favorite brother."

Why hadn't he heard about more of them? Fuck, he didn't think he could deal with another one like Eric and Ellison.

"Is there more of you?"

"You don't have to sound so horrified. But no, it's just me and Sin. Sin isn't here."

"Are you nervous about being alone with me? Be honest, if I don't know how you're feeling, I can't take care of you."

"Yes."

Ellison tried to look away, but he took his boy's pointed chin in his hand. "When you talk to me about things that are bothering you, you will look me in the eyes."

"Okay."

"Tell me why. Talk it out."

"When we were modeling someone hurt me."

Someone other than him touching his boys always pissed him off. The fact he hadn't been there to protect them caused him rage aimed at himself. He knew he didn't have control over what came before, but that didn't change his need to protect Eric and Ellison. Their happiness was his priority.

"He wanted details about what Sin and I did together. I told him nothing, and he wouldn't take no for an answer. He ripped my clothes off. I didn't ask—"

"Ellison, you did nothing wrong. Did he..."

"No, Sin came back."

"I just want you to feel good and make you happy. This is always about you."

"I don't know—"

"Baby, would you like a kiss?"

He needed the bad memories to go away that he'd brought up. He'd never understood people's need to hurt someone they deemed smaller or weaker than themselves. There was a difference between power exchange and consensual sex with a bit of pain. He'd never hurt his boys for anything. Any marks he'd leave on Ellison or Eric would always be welcomed, a sign of who they belonged to.

"Yes, please."

He groaned as his dick got harder at the innocent pink that stained Ellison's cheekbones.

He slipped his arm beneath Ellison and placed his hand on his boy's slim hip. Ellison needed gentleness and to be loved on, that he could do for him. He lowered his mouth to Ellison's, he stroked the softness of the curves, they parted under the pressure of his, and he savored the tiny whimper. Ellison turned his small body into his, and he groaned.

The tiny pair of briefs were the only thing between him and Ellison. He caressed his fingers down the shallow indent of Ellison's spine.

He dipped his fingers into the back of Ellison's briefs and squeezed the soft curves of his boy's cheeks. He didn't try to touch his hole—not even to tease. Ellison was innocent, and his boy had saved it for him. He'd cherish it as long as it was freely given to him.

"What do you want, baby, you name it, and it's yours? All you have to do is ask."

Ellison trembled against him. His boy's chest quickly moved as Ellison tried to catch his breath.

"Say it for me, baby."

The need darkened Ellison's eyes, but the smaller man was also flushed pink with desire and embarrassment. His boy had never asked for what he wanted. He slipped his hand between their bodies and tucked his fingers passed the waistband of Ellison's underwear.

"May I?" he asked as he focused his eyes on Ellison's.

"Please."

"Please what, baby?"

"Daddy."

"Love it when you say it, all breathless and nervous."

He slowly stripped Ellison's briefs down his legs and tossed them over the edge of the bed. He placed his hand on Ellison's chest to keep him flat and studied every inch of his boy. The pale blond curls at the base of Ellison's pretty and slender cock were trimmed. Ellison's balls were hairless.

Ellison kept staring at his cock. "Do you want to touch Daddy's cock?"

"Yes, sir." Ellison arched and whimpered as he cupped and gently squeezed Ellison.

He massaged the firm length until his boy was humping into his palm. He bit, licked and sucked until his boy was marked with beautiful bruises that showed anyone who could see just who Ellison belonged to. Ellison clawed at his back, the pain urged him on, but he needed to do something else first. He rolled onto his back. He'd give Ellison control—the chance to learn his body.

"What, did I do—"

"You did nothing wrong. I want you to touch me, whatever you want to do. I want you to feel safe with me."

"I always feel safe with you."

Ellison looked so sweet as his body lifted to straddle his thighs.

"Daddy, can I..."

"Can you want, baby?"

"Can I suck your cock? I probably won't be good at it."

"This is us. If we make each other feel good, then that's all that matters."

He braced himself as Ellison slid down and warm breath teased the head of his dick. He quickly pushed his hands under his head and linked his fingers. His cock and balls ached, pre-come pooled on his abs, and all he wanted was to bend his boy over and fuck him. Take him hard and fast until his boy begged for more. Fuck him hard enough his boy would feel him for hours—every time Ellison moved or sat down the ache a reminder of what only he could do to and for Ellison.

His body jerked hard at the light and hesitant fingers as Ellison circled the base of his dick. Ellison looked up at him from under long, pale lashes, his boy's pink tongue darted out and licked up the drops at his slit.

"So, good, boy, open your mouth and take just the tip inside."

Ellison did as he bid, the hot, wet suction made him arch his hips off the bed. His boy took more and gagged, spit dripping from the corners of his sexy mouth stretched around his fat cock. Tears filled Ellison's eyes as he tried to take more.

"Easy, baby, take it slow, whatever you do will make Daddy feel good."

His boy shuddered and shallowly bobbed, gagging and moaning. Sweet little needy noises vibrated around his dick. He was so close to fucking coming. He wasn't ready. His boys always came first. He fisted Ellison's baby soft hair and pulled Ellison up as he tightened his abs.

He slammed his mouth against Ellison's, tongue fucking him.

"Daddy, please, it hurts."

"It's okay. I'm going to take such good care of you. Then you're going to turn over, and I'm going to paint that pretty hole. Untouched and innocent, who do you belong to, Ellison?"

"You, only you, Daddy."

He lifted Ellison until his boy's thighs rested on his shoulders. "Place your hands on the wall."

He waited until Ellison did as he instructed and he swallowed Ellison to the root. Soft curls teased his nose, he sucked and swallowed as Ellison bucked and cried out. Nonsense words fell from Ellison's parted lips. His boy smelled so good—so sweet. Ellison tasted perfect on his tongue. He palmed the soft, full curves of Ellison's ass and teased his boy's tight, wrinkled hole with his fingertips.

Ellison's dick jumped and pulsed on his tongue, pre-come flooded his mouth, and he took Ellison all the way to the back of his throat and swallowed. His own cock was so hard it hurt. Soon he'd take care of his own need, but not until he had his boy's seed down his throat.

His boy arched so hard and screamed seconds before his boy lost it, bucking hard. Ellison's slim thighs squeezed his head, and he sucked his boy until Ellison whimpered and tried to push him away.

He lowered Ellison until he let his mouth hover an inch from Ellison's. "Kiss me, find out how good you taste on Daddy's tongue."

The kiss was sweet and shy while Ellison knelt on shaking legs and he took advantage. Reached between them to wrap his hand around his dick. He pushed the head to Ellison's hole, savoring the rhythmic clench as he

81

stroked. Lust was like fire in his veins. Ellison sucked on his tongue.

He threw his head back as his sac tightened, he clenched his hand around his shaft, and the barbells pulled almost painfully under the pressure of his hard strokes.

"One day, I'm going to fuck you, spill every drop inside you. You're going to love Daddy being inside you, won't you? Tell me."

"My ass is only for you, Daddy."

As soon as the last word was out of Ellison's mouth, he spilled onto Ellison's hole. He pushed his mouth to Ellison's as he used the head of his dick to spread his seed around Ellison's hole and along his taint. He'd come so hard he was fucking dizzy. He flipped them onto their sides, Ellison's thigh over his hip, and his boy's wet dick pressed against his abs.

"Such a good boy. You made me so proud. Thank you for trusting me."

"Always," Ellison whispered.

He loved on Ellison, stroked his back and combed his fingers through Ellison's soft hair. Kissed him gently between words of praise. His boys, both of them were everything he'd wanted and needed but had denied himself. He wasn't doing that any longer.

"Let's go take a shower and I'll get you all clean, then get you coffee and breakfast."

He didn't wait for an answer just slipped off the bed, picked Ellison up and carried him to the bathroom. He slowly washed Ellison's smooth skin. He brought him to another release before he let the sleepy and satisfied boy head to the kitchen for coffee.

10 Flying Was Where He Felt Like Himself

Saint soared miles above the ground. His *Cessna* in perfect shape. This was where he felt like himself, confident in his abilities. Everyone had that one thing that they excelled at, and this was his. When he flew, it was normally just him and the open sky in all directions. Ernie understood that was his freedom. The one place he had control.

"Saint, you copy?"

"Go ahead, Ernie."

"I'm patching a call through."

"Thanks, Ernie." He heard the crackle in his ears before a voice that made him smile filled his head.

"Hey, baby, how's my Ellison?"

"Doing good, Mama. I thought you were out of radio range." The last time he'd talked to his mama she was headed into the mountains for a two-week survivalist trip. She loved her job, and as much as they wanted her around more often, it was understood she didn't want to settle down. When she'd lost their dad, he believed she lost her soulmate, and no other man would do. Outside of sex, he didn't think his mother really liked men.

"Stupid egos and a broken leg."

"Did he break it or did you break it for him?"

He listened to her snort as he turned to head back to the airfield. His lunch break was almost up.

"He broke it, but it was a close one to me taking out his kneecaps. Ernie said you went up by yourself, so what's up? You and Eric are always together, you fly, and he jumps."

"I just needed quiet."

"Why? Is this about your man? Ernie was telling me you were seeing that Sheriff you and your brother have been panting over."

"I don't know, it's odd. I didn't think it would work out and it seems to be." Years of wanting someone, it overwhelmed him that Camden finally agreed to be theirs. He held their hands in public. He showed them affection with others around. They weren't kept a secret, and they'd stayed out at his house the past few weeks. Camden made sure he spent time alone with either him or Sin. It was blowjobs and hand jobs, but beyond that Camden hadn't pushed for anything else. As much as he appreciated Camden taking it slow, the longer he was with the man, the more he wanted to know what Camden felt like inside him. Yes, he was terrified, but Camden would never hurt him or Sin.

"That's good, you and Eric deserve this. Someone who will love you both. You know I told you and your brother when you said you'd find a man to share that the perfect one would come along."

"I know, Mama."

"Since I'm grounded for a bit, and I don't have any trips planned, I thought I'd come for a visit."

"That would be great."

"And I can meet Camden. Check out this boy y'all are dating."

"Mama, please don't call him a boy, he's the same age as you."

"Then I'll be able to meet your old man then."

"Mama, please don't call him an old man when you meet him."

"What can I say to him? This man is dating my precious sons. The least you'll allow me is the opportunity to interrogate him and ask his intentions. I'll try to be all nice and polite if that will make you and Eric happy."

He laughed at her disgusted tone when she said she'd try to be nice and polite. "It's the best I can hope for."

"Don't be so pessimistic, Ellison."

"I'll try. I'm about to land."

"Okay, sweetie, tell your brother I said I love him. I love you too, Ellison. Everything will work out."

The call was ended, and he circled as he prepared to land. He descended as he aimed for the short runway. He pulled back as he slowed and smoothly went wheels down, then he taxied closer to one of the two hangers. Killing the engine, he removed his headset and hopped out of his plane.

"How was it?" Ernie asked.

"Perfect."

He turned to study Ernie. He'd wondered what his mother saw in the man. Ernie and his mama weren't compatible. They'd shared a bed for a few years, but the sex seemed all that the two people shared in common.

Ernie was decked out in his usual oil-stained coveralls. A chewed cigar between his lips. Ernie never seemed to light the ever-present item. It was as a part of Ernie as the coveralls.

"You love to fly, I know that, but you don't normally come without Sin."

"Were you talking to Mama?"

"Anyone who knows you, knows you two boys are attached. So, what's bothering you?"

"I don't know. Everything seems to be going good, ya know, I'm just waiting for the punch."

"Ellison, not everything falls through. Sometimes people just get their happy ending without going through all the bullshit. You been checking out that Pelter guy since he came to town. Waiting around that long, maybe that's the punch, and now all the good shit comes now."

"Thanks, Ernie."

"I know shit didn't go right with your mom and me, but that wasn't destined to last. Layla and me had our moment, and we both moved on. But I loved you boys. You were the best thing I got out of that relationship. Now, get your ass to work. Sin will be wondering where you at."

He gave Ernie a quick hug and strode toward the car. He felt lighter now that he'd had his time alone. It had always been him and Sin. Always a package. Sin had had his dates, but him, he didn't have anything of his own. He hadn't realized it. Yes, he couldn't be separated from Sin, and he wouldn't want to be. Things were different since Camden claimed them. Camden treated them as separate people. He made them feel special with his time and attention, even when it was the three of them together.

He sighed as he drove toward the main road and back toward town. Camden understood and gave them what they needed. He wished Camden would let them in more. Where he was attentive with them, it was as if Camden didn't require or even think he deserved the same in return.

He and Sin wanted to give those things to Camden. Be there when he got home from work or a middle of the night talk when he gets called away. They wanted it all, but they had to get Camden to realize that they loved and wanted him—to take care of him just like he did them.

He put aside the thoughts as he pulled into town and turned off the main drag to Pleasure. After work, they'd go to Camden's place and spend time with their man. Everything would work out like it should; he just had to keep believing that.

11 This Was the Life

Sin hummed as he moved through the aisles of Pleasure and straightened the shelves. Saint was at his usual post at the register working on the endless list of website updates Fred hated to do. They'd spent the last three days at Camden's house only leaving to go to work. Camden made them dinner every night. Then he tucked them into bed beside him every night. That was the life he'd imagined with the three of them.

Camden was surprisingly attentive and affectionate with them. Kisses, hugs, and cuddling, but no sex. It was odd, men had tried to fuck him and Saint for years and the man they loved didn't seem to be in a hurry. Odd but nice.

The moaning sounded signaling a customer, and he stood on his tiptoes to peek over one of the shelves. Pure walked in, and the big man had a smile on his handsome face. The former SWAT sniper and now bounty hunter/bodyguard was a massive cutie. Even with stubble, the man was downright pretty.

"Look at this, our number one customer." He ran toward Pure and threw his arms around the man's waist.

"I don't come here that often."

"You so do. What are you here to replace Raul with?"

"I'm not replacing Raul because there is no Raul and me."

He sucked his teeth and shook his head. Since Raul came to work for Trenton Security on a more full-time basis, Pure upped his usual shopping trips. Pure thought he hid his interest, but the man sucked at not drooling over the hot bounty hunter.

"Lie to everyone else including yourself, but we've seen the porn videos you've bookmarked."

Pure went bright red, and he chuckled at the big man.

"Stay away from my laptop, and you're never invited to my house again."

"You should password protect that bitch."

"Pure, what are you looking for today?" Saint asked with a smile and walked out from behind the counter.

"Saint at least doesn't want to embarrass me."

"I don't want to embarrass you. Raul is pretty hot."

"He's okay," Pure muttered and walked off.

"Leave Pure alone. Raul will make him give in sooner or later."

"That is true, Raul has been awful interrogate-y since he found out Pure comes here."

"Camden texted and said he wouldn't be home until late. He said we didn't have to stay at the house tonight."

"Of course we're going to be there."

Things weren't perfect, but this wasn't some fairy tale bullshit. Camden felt right to them, and they'd decided they were all in. Camden needed them, and they'd be there. He understood the man's need for space. What was happening between them was new and as such they'd have a lot of trial and error before they found the right routine for them.

"We don't get out of here until eight, and we need to make a stop at the house for clothes."

"You do know, Saint, Camden prefers us naked."

"I have no idea why he insists on us being nude while he walks around the house fully clothed in that damn uniform of his. It's fucking torture."

He giggled as his annoyed brother stormed off. To be honest, he thought Camden had the naked rule more for Saint's benefit. His twin was confident or at least faked it well, around their friends, but he was still unsure around Camden. Except for the weight difference they were exactly the same, and over the years, Saint grew to despise the comparison made between them. Being identical twins made it difficult to be considered separate entities.

Their man filled out a uniform, but it wasn't as sexy as the black tactical gear Camden wore the night shit went nuclear out at Brawlers and the old, corrupt Sheriff ended up dead. It wasn't love at first sight but lust for sure. The more time they'd had with Camden, the stories they'd heard, they'd quickly come to see the man as more than a jerk-off fantasy. Finally, they had him, and they weren't going to fuck it up.

That started with them showing Camden they didn't give a shit about the age difference.

He went back to work. The night passed quickly with a steady stream of customers and a few friends coming in to hang out. Pleasure wasn't a booming business in a town like Powers, but the website saved their asses. Their mama said they could come back to work for her, but as exciting as the travel and adrenaline were, it would keep them away from Camden and their friends. He and Saint talked about a change of scenery over the years. Yet this is where they belonged and were safe.

He walked from the back after stashing the night deposit in the safe and found Saint stowing the laptop under the counter. They worked together as they turned off all the lights, set the alarm and locked the door. They joined arms as they walked toward their house. It was a short walk, but they liked the fresh air after being cooped up inside most of the day.

"Do you think if everything works out, Camden might like a ceremony like Elijah had with his men?"

"I don't know, should we go look at rings?"

"No, I was just thinking, ya know?"

He tugged Saint off balance, and his twin stumbled against him. "I know, you also went out yesterday on your break to fly. So, what's on your mind?"

"He hasn't tried to have—"

"Sex isn't all about penetration."

"I know that, and I get it, but—"

"There're no buts here. We've got our man, sleeping beside him every night. Can't get much better than that. So, we'll go with the flow, and it'll work out just like it's supposed to. Let's go to the house, pack a bag for the evening and clothes for work. We'll go home and make Camden dinner."

"Home? Camden might not appreciate us taking over his house."

"He did give us a key."

"Very true. Implies we can come and go as we please."

They walked up the cracked sidewalk and let themselves into their house. They moved out of Ernie's place at eighteen and rented their house. Peaches definitely didn't charge them as much as she probably should for the house. It was a way for them to have independence and they appreciated it, even though they argued to pay regular rent over the last few years.

Peaches would just smile and say they'd have a new place soon.

"Should we just pack a bag for a few nights instead of coming here before work every day?"

"Let's pack. Oh, did I tell you Mama's coming to visit?"

"Shit, no. When did you talk to Mama?"

"Ernie patched her through while I was in the air yesterday."

Their mama wasn't the easiest woman to get along with. She was opinionated and crazy, and she knew nothing about personal space or boundaries. She was like Lucky's mom. They loved her, but some people couldn't get past the outspokenness.

"We're going to have to tell Camden."

"When he comes home tonight. Let's get packed."

They stuffed a bag full of clothes and personal items into a duffel. It didn't take long to get on the road. Making a stop at the grocery store for things they were low on and quickly headed out of town. He and Saint relaxed at the same time as they pulled into the long driveway. It was home. It felt right.

They parked and headed inside. Saint headed for the kitchen, and he headed upstairs to put their bag in the bedroom. They hadn't made the bed before they left that morning. He set the bag down.

He loved Saint more than himself most days. His twin was the only reason he got out of bed. He'd tried to be the strong one, put himself between Saint and the bullies—

between everyone who had wanted to hurt Saint. Accepting the bruises and all the things he couldn't change to make sure Saint was okay. The night he let the wrong man near him, the bastard had thought he was Saint, and he'd pretended. He'd kept that secret, and he'd told Camden part of it. For once he'd felt safe being with Camden. Secure that tomorrow would be okay and the day after, all the ones that followed.

"Sin, come help me with dinner."

"Coming, I'm just straightening the bed."

"Well hurry up, Camden texted he's on his way here after some meeting. I told him we were home."

Camden would be home soon. He quickly made the bed but left it turned down. He kicked off his shoes and went to help Saint with dinner.

12 Why Couldn't His Quiet Town Stay Fucking Quiet?

The reports were opened on his desk, and it was all bullshit. The deceased Sheriff Thorpe was as big a pain in the ass dead as when the bastard was alive. The files weren't really meant for him, but he'd called in a few favors when he'd heard there was activity out at the old Thorpe place which was butted up to Joker Webb's property. All of it was out in the middle of bumfuck, nowhere. Miles and miles of woods to search. He'd kept this shit quiet as long as he could, but he needed backup, and the only team he trusted was Trenton Security.

Also, Linus and his crew typically skirted the law, and he wanted to be prepared if they needed to run an operation off the books. Human Trafficking was a scourge and one that he didn't see them ever eradicating completely. Yet every little bit helped, and if it was one or fifty, he'd call it a semi-win.

"Why is it when I think everything is going pretty damn good, you call with bad fucking news?"

He looked up to find Linus standing in his doorway.

"If I didn't have to call, I wouldn't have."

"I know. I had Hunter run the information before I left the office. Turns out Thorpe had more partners than we knew about. When he died, it was our fuck up not to check that his accounts were quickly emptied and closed. Where the money went, my guess is it disappeared into the ether."

"I don't know if they're using Thorpe's property as a weigh station and transferring from there or a lay low point."

"My guess, they're too cocky and think no one will be out there checking shit out."

"Probably, but, man—"

"You don't trust your old team or someone connected to them."

"Shit just wasn't adding up before I left. It wasn't that the guys got flashy with the shit. They weren't taking extravagant vacations, didn't show up with new cars, but my team is smart. They've been taking down corrupt cops for years. It's what our unit was designed for. If anyone knows how to hide their dirty dealings, it's them."

"They can only hide so much. My team doesn't play by the rules and we sure as fuck don't stand down when told. Everyone's in. I called in Raul, and Gage is ready to make us look good if this falls through. Not to mention Peaches called in a few favors."

"Peaches? The last guy Peaches had me talk to terrified even me. I felt like I should've been at the meeting with riot gear on."

"Vinnie was a sweetheart." Peaches peeked around Linus.

She stepped into his office. She wore a fitted three-piece suit, and her hair was in a conservative twist. It hid her thread wraps and the tiny bells in her blond curls.

"Vinnie had mafia written all over him."

"Come on. He just had some youthful indiscretions."

To Peaches, the law wasn't black and white—she lived in the gray areas. He couldn't fault her for it. It made her one of the best defense attorneys in the country. She worked her ass off to rehabilitate her clients and the ones she couldn't. They made perfect allies down the road.

"He ran guns."

"Everyone needs to eat, Camden." She took one of the chairs in front of his desk and crossed her legs, and then she leaned back to smile at him serenely.

"And why am I not surprised you said that?"

"Because you're an exceptionally brilliant man, who has two young men waiting for him at home and you're in the office."

"I did hire on as a Sheriff after you tracked me down and told me I was taking the job, which means I'm here to work."

"You're going to go home to your men."

He swore the crew ladies thought they were his only bosses and knew way too much about his life. If he didn't adore his men so much, he'd run back to Atlanta and the state police in a second.

"And how do you know they're at my house?"

"I'm their landlord and live across the street. They haven't been home."

"Do you often stalk your tenants?"

"Only the ones I've adopted. Also, that neighbor of theirs is a nightmare. You should really do something about her."

"I barely pay attention to her complaints and how did we get off the subject of human traffickers and onto my love life?"

"Because we already set up a meeting at Trenton Headquarters for Friday. So that's taken care of. Now, you need to take care of your men. I don't want to deal with two sweet brokenhearted boys when they realize how much of an asshole their boyfriend is."

"I'm not an asshole."

"You are, and you need those boys to love you before they realize it. You're not all that pretty, Camden, I mean, yeah, you're handsome and have your charm, but really, do you think—"

"They're mine, Peaches."

"Then fucking act like it."

"I take them out. I don't hide we're together in public. I'm doing everything I can to let them know I care about them. Aren't you going to help me out here, Trenton?"

He glared at Linus who was smugly grinning at him from beside the door. When did his life come down to nosy as fuck friends and mother figures who thought he was an unworthy asshole who couldn't get his men to love him? These people were going to start making him drink and not socially.

"Oh no, you're on your own, we depend on her to keep us out of jail. She has more authority than you do."

"Then what the hell do you suppose I do?"

"Maybe sex, because as uptight are you are, I swear you ain't getting any. Do you need some, you know, get-it-up pills? Because they're easy enough to get. I can make an appointment with a doctor for you. It's not something to be ashamed of, a man of your age and all that and with two twenty-something young men. They have needs, Camden."

He clenched his jaw at Peaches' innocent, motherly expression like she wasn't talking about his supposed impotence. It wasn't helping Linus was about to piss himself or have a heart attack from his laughter. He was rethinking this whole new life and friends thing. He'd rather be shot at every day.

"Nothing is wrong with my dick. It works just fine."

"From your crankiness, I very much doubt it."

"I'm going the fuck home."

"Camden, I said this wasn't something to be ashamed of. You're a man of a certain age, and sometimes things no longer work like they're supposed to, and it's perfectly natural."

"How has Gib stayed married to you as long as he has?"

"The sex is amazing. He's never had—" She leaned in and whispered, "—your problem, but I'm sure he wouldn't—"

"Get out!" He stormed around the desk, gently lifted Peaches from the chair and ushered her out his office door. Not too gently, he shoved the braying, red-faced Linus out behind her.

"If you need to talk about your problem I'm only—"

He slammed the door and dropped his head back to stare at the ceiling. He needed new friends, maybe a new job in Antarctica. He'd heard Elijah had looked into running away. Maybe he still had the info.

He wanted sex with his boys, but they'd both been treated harshly by men in the past—one who wouldn't take no for an answer and another who didn't take the time to love on Eric the way he should've. Being your lover's first was an honor and should be treated as such.

He checked the time, and it was already later than he'd planned. He'd texted Ellison almost two hours ago that he'd be home after his meeting. The meeting hadn't gone as he expected and ended with his ability to please his boys questioned. After he grabbed his keys and leather jacket, he strode toward the door and hoped like hell Peaches and Linus were gone. He couldn't deal with round two.

He wanted to take his boys on a real date. He'd had them to the house for dinner and bought them dinner at the diner, but they deserved one at a fancy restaurant or maybe a night out of Powers. Trouble and Brody had this place they went to, and it sounded perfect.

On his way to his vehicle, he pulled out his phone and scrolled for Trouble's number.

"I didn't do it."

He chuckled at Trouble's voice. The man had to be one of the normal ones which really wasn't saying much. He thought about the group of people he'd met since moving there.

Landon and Zerk were crazy, and embarrassment ensued when he was trapped somewhere with them. Scary, Elijah, and Tank were close to being booked for indecent exposure. He'd caught them one too many times with Elijah bent over one of their bikes. He didn't know how the man put up with Scary and Tank, well, more Scary.

Lucky and Priest might be weird, but at least when they were together, they were completely focused on each other. Crave and poor Twitch…he didn't know how Twitch could walk. Psycho and Ben, those two were a weird little family with Psycho's ex-wife and her current wife, and their three kids were out there. He couldn't deny everyone loved each other unconditionally.

"You're one of the only ones I haven't thought about busting. No, you and Brody were talking about some bed and breakfast. I wanted to do something nice for Eric and Ellison."

"You want a romantic place?"

"Yeah, and since you two go, I thought it would be gay couple friendly."

"It's definitely that. Brody found it, and some of the other guys have taken their men there too. Scary and Tank even took Elijah a few times. So, triads aren't an issue. Want me to text you the details? They're great about making it romantic. I'm not so great about that shit."

"You seem to keep your man happy."

"Brody and Princess are my everything, man. He took a chance, and I'll never be able to let him know how much I appreciate that."

He smiled at the obvious love Trouble had for his husband of seven years. All the stories he'd heard about Trouble and Brody, Trouble had gone all-out on making Brody his. It was almost like one of those romance novels. A story you sure as fuck never believed was true. It was that way with all his friends and their partners.

"I'm sure he knows, he's stuck with you for seven years."

"I know right. Fuck, I didn't think I'd get one date and when he said yes…no fucking way I was screwing that up."

"Just text me all the info. I better get home to Eric and Ellison."

"So it's true, you got them out at your place. The rumors have been flying about the Sheriff and his pretty boys. Strange for someone who avoided Sin and Saint like the plague."

"I had a few things to work through."

"No problem, man. I'm just glad it worked out for you. You gotta come out for our next run. We keep asking."

"I know, maybe one Sunday soon."

"Don't make me send Princess and Juvie after you. They can be kinda terrifying."

"I get that. No need to sic the Crew Hellions on me."

He loved the kids. He saw them as guests of his jail one day, but they were the Crew's kids, so that wasn't too surprising.

"I better get home. They probably expected me an hour ago or more."

"I'll get you the details here shortly."

"I appreciate it, Trouble."

"Not a problem. Got to keep our partners happy."

"Exactly." He disconnected the call and got into his vehicle. Since Eric and Ellison had started staying with him, he hadn't been going to bed or getting up as early as he typically did. His life didn't revolve around his job, but he knew that he might be giving them mixed signals. If there were things he needed to fix, that was the biggest one.

What he felt for them was more than he had for anyone in the past and he needed them to understand that. This was so far out of his comfort zone he was lost. That wasn't going to keep his boys happy, and he wanted nothing more than to have them with him. He needed a better balance in his life. It wasn't about just his job anymore.

He turned onto his drive and pulled up to his house. The porch light was on, and the place looked bright, welcoming, and that was because the twins were inside waiting for him. He loved coming home to them there, and when he'd texted earlier saying they didn't have to come over, he'd hoped they would. He needed to know they wanted to be there. He turned off the engine just as the front door opened.

A small smile pulled at the corner of his mouth at the sight of Ellison and Eric waiting for him. He hopped out and jogged up to the house. When he neared them, he pulled them into his arms. He hugged them close as he walked them back into the house. He wanted to get used to that feeling, and he wasn't giving it up no matter how many doubts filled his head.

13 Camden Was Being Weird

Camden had worked his ass off the last few weeks. The man didn't like talking about his work when he came home, and they hadn't pushed for details. That morning after nights of he and Sin going to bed alone for weeks, Camden woke them up to tell them to pack for a weekend away. Camden didn't do weekend trips, and he seemed fidgety—a little unsure.

"Are you going to share where we're going?" Sin asked from the passenger seat.

He turned to watch Camden and waited for the man to answer. The incessant *are we there yet* hadn't gotten them the answers they'd wanted, but each one made Camden smile.

"We're almost there. It'll just be another half hour. Don't you two ever get surprises?"

"No. Mama was so bad at it she told us our Christmas presents just so she didn't have to wrap them."

"When's she coming to visit again?"

He and Sin looked at each other amused by the man's obvious discomfort at meeting their mama.

"A trip fell through, and she'd planned to arrive this coming week, but something came up so she'll be here in a few more weeks. She blocked out the time."

"Do you think she'll like me? She's going to hate me. I'm the same age—"

"Actually, you're three years older than Mama," he supplied, and it earned him a snort from Sin.

Camden had relaxed about the age difference, but he'd told them he'd never met parents before. That shocked him since he'd assumed Camden had at least a few semi-serious relationships in his past. They'd learned a lot about Camden. The man never shied away from answering their questions. Camden's parents weren't accepting of him being gay. They'd asked would they be able to meet them, and when Camden explained, they'd quickly forgotten the idea. Camden said he didn't celebrate, but he wanted to spend the holidays with his boys.

"Great, thank you for sharing that." Camden groaned and scrubbed his hand over his face.

"Quit being so sensitive about it. Mama doesn't care. She might make some old man jokes, but we told you how she is."

"I'd kinda like for my boyfriends' mother to like me."

Sin turned back around to wink at him between the seats, and he covered his smile.

"She'll love you, promise."

They lapsed into silence, and he watched the scenery blur by outside the window. They'd crossed the Florida line about fifteen minutes before. He tried to think back to their conversations. Camden asked about everything, what they liked, hated, what they wanted to do besides work at

Pleasure. He loved his job, Sin did too, and they couldn't really see themselves doing anything else. They liked people. They helped people find things to make them feel good and sexy.

"Did y'all do okay with Loco—"

"His name is Ezekiel, for only a few months, he's a little crazy, but most babies are," Sin protested.

Mary was their friend Joker's mother, and she'd just given birth to a baby boy a few months ago. They'd offered to babysit so Mary and her husband Bear could have a night to themselves since everything had healed up. Ezekiel went a little loco when Mary got out of his sight too long, but he'd been such a good baby when he'd spent the night with them.

"It's a perfect nickname and don't you all get them?"

"Yeah, but come on, we already have Rage and Gunner, Juvie and Princess, Peace, but Peace is Matty's middle name. Craig's starting to be called Pride. Can't the next generation of our craziness at least have normal names?"

"Baby, what about y'all and the crews is normal?"

"Ouch, Mr. Pelter. Are you saying your perfect boyfriends aren't normal?" Sin asked.

"Do I have to answer that?"

They both smacked Camden's arm, and he chuckled.

"Don't take out the fact y'all were saddled with nicknames on me."

"Saint, don't you think our so-called boyfriend needs a nickname?"

"No, I don't need a nickname. You two can call me Camden, and the others can call me Pelter like they've always done. Here we are," Camden announced as they pulled off onto a dirt road that led into a vineyard.

He glanced out all the windows. An old Victorian-style house stood in the distance behind a large stone mansion. It was rolling hills and blue sky, and it was beautiful. Camden pulled past the large house and into the parking spots in front of the house.

"What's this?"

"Trouble brings Brody here for anniversaries. I called, and they luckily had a spot open for a weekend. Someone had canceled. I wanted to take you someplace nice, just the three of us, nobody popping in at odd hours."

"It's gorgeous, thank you." Saint removed his seat belt and leaned into the front seat to kiss Camden then got out as Sin threw himself into Camden's lap.

On some level, he'd thought he'd compare himself to Sin if they shared the same man, but he didn't, not since dinner at Camden's house months ago. Camden treated them differently. He wasn't taking Sin's place when his twin wasn't around. The big man wanted them both. He ambled around to the front, and Camden and Sin joined him. The big man took both their hands and led them up the cobblestone walkway.

"Mr. Pelter." An older gentleman with steel-gray hair and a friendly smile on his bearded face stepped out onto the porch.

"Yes, please call me Camden, Lowell. This Eric and Ellison."

"Pleasure to meet you three. Please, come in, and I'll get you all checked in, then show you to your room."

Lowell kept up a steady stream of conversation as he showed them around as they moved to the office at the back of the house. It was very nice, perfectly decorated, but still felt like someone's home.

"Once you're checked in, the house is yours. We pride ourselves on offering our guests a romantic getaway when it's couples or triads, and also a place for families to get together. I have a small cottage out back, if you need anything, don't hesitate to call."

"So, you don't stay in the house?"

He stood back as he let Camden and the other man talk, and he locked arms with Sin. He'd never expected a romantic weekend getaway thing. He and Sin talked about all the trips their friends took. They just never tried to assume they'd have something normal—well, normal for them.

"I do on occasion, but no, with guest such as yourself we offer as much privacy as possible. I'll be by in the morning around nine to make breakfast." The man typed away, and then the printer came to life with a few sheets of paper coming out. "There's a restaurant in the winery where you can get lunch or dinner. If you pull back out onto the main road, there's a small town if you'd like to purchase something we don't offer. The kitchen is stocked with plenty of snacks and drinks. Just sign these and I'll show you to your room."

"Thank you very much. I know I was lucky someone canceled."

"It happens, and it's very much last minute. We always love to have our calendar full with guests."

Camden and Lowell spoke as Camden signed all the paperwork and accepted a key. They followed Lowell up to a third-floor room with a large brass bed. The windows faced the front and overlooked the vines. Lowell told them goodbye with assurances to call if they needed anything and to come by his cottage and he'd lead them to the winery for a tour.

As they stared out the window, he felt as unsure as his twin, and it was odd. This was all new, and he didn't know what to expect. Camden wrapped his arms around them from behind.

"So, what do you think? Did I do okay because you two are awful quiet."

Sin nudged him, and he darted a glance at his twin. "No one has ever taken us away for a weekend before."

"You're a little out of your comfort zone. I should've asked, I'm—"

"No, don't be sorry. It's perfect, and it's really nice."

Camden kissed the tops of their heads, and they leaned back into him.

"I know work's been a bitch lately, and I'm sorry we haven't been able to spend a lot of time together. Being stuck out at my place can't be fun."

"We love your place," they said in unison.

"But I haven't exactly been the best boyfriend or partner whatever you want to call me. I'm new to all this, and I want it to work out."

"I think I can speak for Saint and myself...we want this to work out too. So, what's the plan?"

"No plan. Just the three of us hanging out. I'm not much of a wine drinker, but I thought what the hell. The website said there're shops nearby. We can drink wine. Just spend time without me having to go to the office. I even left my work phone at home. If an emergency does come up everyone knows how to get in touch."

"No phone? No midnight calls? Just the three of us?" Saint released Sin's arm, and they turned to look up at Camden.

"I promise, Wren and the rest of the deputies can handle everything. This weekend is about us."

It sounded so perfect. Camden's big hand curled around the back of his neck and Camden lowered his mouth to his. It was instant hard-on every time. He didn't understand how a simple kiss could turn him on so quickly. Camden's tongue pushed passed his lips, and he moaned as he lifted onto his toes. He fisted his hands in Camden's t-shirt. The kiss slowly ended, and then Camden turned to Sin, repeating the actions. A few more quick kisses and Camden stepped back taking their hands.

"Let's go get our bags and head to the winery for dinner and drinks. Then we'll come back here. How's that sound."

He nodded, and like always, Camden didn't pull away from them. He looked at them like he was proud that they were his. He didn't worry about what was going on at home. He just wanted to spend time with Camden and Sin. This was his family—the three of them.

14 It Was Almost Like a Fairy Tale

He'd drank enough wine to have a slight buzz, so he just felt warm. Camden had been a gentleman all night. Pulled out their chairs. Refilled their glasses and they'd talked about everything and nothing. Dinner was amazing, and they were walking back into the bed and breakfast. He and Saint held hands as Camden unlocked the door and stepped back to let them go first. Camden had touched them all night. Small caresses to their lower backs, held their hands and kissed them whenever the big man felt like it. He knew he'd tensed the first few times and sensed Saint had too, but no one had seemed to pay them any attention.

The dining room had filled up as they were finishing dinner. He emptied his wineglass and placed it on the counter as he passed.

"Go on upstairs. I'm going to lock up and be right there."

He turned to smile over his shoulder at Camden. His arms and legs felt heavy. The wine had relaxed him, and even Saint seemed to be mellower than normal. He loved Saint, but his twin had a tendency to be a little high-strung when he was nervous.

They slowly ascended the steps to their room. The door stood open, and he swore they'd closed it before they left. Shimmering lights illuminated the room, and when he walked inside, his gasp was mirrored by his brother's. Electric candles filled the room. The bed was turned down.

"I know you two probably didn't need all the candlelight and all, but I wanted to give that to y'all."

He turned as he and Saint separated. "Why?"

"Well, since it's y'all's first time, I wanted to make it special. Am I being a total moron right now?"

"No," he and Saint bellowed.

"It's perfect. No one ever thought to romance us before." He turned to see the awe on Saint's face at what Camden had done for them.

"I thought you two deserved it. Now, I want you two to do something for me." Camden's eyes turned dark, and the man removed his t-shirt.

Every muscle was tight. They knew Camden worked out with Liv and Little at least three days a week and sparred with the Trenton Crew the other two.

"Strip."

He darted a nervous glance at Saint. He hadn't heard that commanding tone since the night he'd showered with Camden.

"I want you two naked and on the bed."

They quickly stripped as Camden walked over to his bag. He straightened with condoms and a bottle of lube in his hands. They went to the bed and lay down.

"We need to talk, if either of you don't want this, you always have the right to tell me no. I don't care if I'm balls deep, you tell me to stop, and it ends there, no questions asked. Do you understand?"

"Yes." Both their voices cracked as they answered.

They'd prepared every day for this moment. Every time Camden had sucked his dick and played with his ass, he'd asked himself would he finally know what it was like to be fucked by the big man, but each time Camden made him feel good and took the bare minimum for himself. He and Saint talked about it, Camden made every touch special and never demanded. They wondered if Camden even knew how to be selfish.

Camden avoided relationships so that he'd never leave someone behind. Told them it wasn't fair, but they knew that minutes, hours or years weren't guaranteed. They'd learned that they needed to accept the time they had and enjoy it, love hard because it wouldn't always be there.

The condoms and lube were tossed onto the bed, then Camden stripped. He took in how the light played over the dark skin that covered the strength beneath. Every shift and play of powerful muscles. Camden was built like a man that made other's insecure about how they looked, but Camden made them feel gorgeous. Camden's gaze moved over him, then Saint before Camden crawled into bed. The mattress dipped under his weight.

Then it was a full-on assault, kisses and touches, sharp bites and sucks until they were arched off the bed. He'd learned Camden loved leaving marks, touching or kissing them later to remind them of the pleasure and pain. Saint gasped, and he opened his eyes to find Camden sucking Saint's cock. The backs of Saint's thighs on Camden's shoulders. Camden bobbed and played between Saint's thighs. The snick of the lube, and seconds later, Saint writhed and begged.

He lifted to his knees and came up behind Camden. He stroked his mouth along the man's spine, licked the salty taste from Camden's skin.

As Camden lifted, he wrapped his arms around Camden and took his thick cock in his hand. He peeked around Camden to see Saint holding his legs open. He played with the barbells, caught them with his nails and listened to Camden growl.

"Fuck, so sweet and sexy, innocent and all fucking mine. Tell me yes, baby."

Saint stuttered out a yes.

Camden's hands came back to squeeze his cheeks and finger his hole. "Eric, I want you on your back and getting yourself all nice and ready, because I'm not stopping until both my boys come on my cock."

He nearly lost it on Camden's ass at the words. He didn't realize he'd closed his eyes until Camden's fingers tightened in his hair and pulled him around until Camden's mouth slammed down on his. The kiss was brutal, not gentle like the others, so this wasn't like the times before.

He was pushed onto his back and watched Camden roll a condom on. Camden used the lube and afterward pressed the bottle into his hand.

Camden lay down on Saint, the man stroked Saint's cheeks, and Camden's left hand pushed between them.

"Baby, I want you to keep breathing, and then I need you to push out for me. Can you do that?"

"Yes."

"Don't be scared, this is about you, you come first, always."

He watched Saint's face closely, waited for the fear or a flash of pain, but Saint's eyes widened.

"Breath, baby, that's right. Such a good boy. You like me fucking you?"

He watched the slow, fluid motions of Camden, the way Camden's muscles contracted and released. Camden spoke to Saint in a low tone, most of it too quiet for him to hear. Saint whimpered, and Camden grunted.

He let his eyes close as he slicked his fingers and prepared himself for Camden. He listened to the sounds, the smell of sex that thickened in the room and felt the motion of the bed. The sway quickened and slowed in a teasing rhythm. He peeked from under his lashes to find Camden watching him.

"Turn sideways. I want to suck your cock as you get yourself ready."

He obeyed with his fingers deep in his ass, and he nearly screamed as Camden swallowed his cock. He didn't know what was going on, so he focused on Camden sucking him. He thrust two fingers, then three until he reached four as he pounded into his ass. Camden's goatee was tickling his nuts and taint. Then a scream had him opening his eyes to find Saint arched off the bed, come covering his belly and Camden pulled away to kiss the tears from Saint's lashes and cheeks. Camden's thrusts were shallow as he drew out Saint's pleasure.

"Love how you come on my fat dick. So, fucking tight. Letting me love on that ass…only mine. Tell me, Ellison, you belong to me, only me."

"Only you."

"My good boy, baby."

The caresses weren't hurried. Camden wasn't rushing from Saint to him. Camden was gentle and sweet, everything Saint needed.

Camden pulled back slowly, sat back on his heels and removed the condom, then replaced it with a new one.

"On your knees." Camden's order punctuated with hands gently turning him over. "Shit, look at the pretty ass."

Camden landed a few smacks, and Sin threw his head back, the pleasure and pain he'd learned he loved from Camden. Camden bit at his throat as the thick head pushed into his hole. The barbells felt odd as they flipped over his rim. He bit his lip as they teased his prostate. The thrusts were shallow, going deeper on every slid inside. Saint moaned, and he turned his head to see Camden had Saint lifted with a hand behind his head.

Camden and Saint kissed as Camden fucked him harder. Camden's fingers laced through his left, and he noticed Camden released Saint and held his twin's hand.

The big man's attention came back fully to him. The press of their mouths was awkward, all tongue and teeth with labored breaths. His ass was on fire with the brutal jabs and the slap of Camden's hips against him. Camden released his hand then wrapped his fingers around the front of his throat.

"So beautiful, such a good boy, taking my cock. Show your Daddy how much you love it. Fuck yourself on my dick. I want to watch you take it."

His cock jerked, and he looked over his shoulder. Camden knelt behind him. The man's focus on where he was embedded in his ass. He thrust back, ground against the man and felt the course pubes against his hole, he repeated the thrust and grind until he couldn't take it anymore. He rode the thick, pierced length of Camden cock harder and faster. Camden's fingers fisted in his hair.

"That's right, boy. Come on my cock. Then I'll let you and Ellison taste when I come. Give it to me, boy."

The hard slap to his ass had him reaching for his cock, and he stroked until the pleasure was so painful he could barely touch himself until he came on the sheet under him. His body bowed and then Camden was gone, and he was thrown onto his back.

Camden stroked his bare cock above his and Saint's face.

"My beautiful boys, waited so—" A grunt turned into a growl. "—long for you two to be mine. Open your mouths."

He opened his mouth just as Camden came. He whimpered at the salty, bitter taste on his tongue, but he couldn't look away. Camden's back was bowed, his sweat glistened in the flickering light as he brutally stroked his cock painting their faces with his release.

Camden's mouth was on his, tongue fucking his mouth, then Saint's. Camden fell between them, pulled them close until their heads rested on Camden's wide heaving chest.

His ass was sore, and he could barely keep his eyes open, but he turned to check Saint. His twin was smiling with his eyes closed. Blissed out and happy, the most relaxed he'd ever seen Saint.

"You two were so good. Boys, did I make you two feel good."

"Yes, Daddy."

A kiss brushed his forehead then Saint's. He didn't think he could get any happier. He was right where he wanted to be, and it might not be a fairy tale, but it was fucking close.

15 He'd Arrest Linus If He Didn't Need the Bastard

Camden had counted to ten so much he'd probably reached five hundred, and he'd only arrived at Trenton Security an hour ago. Liv was all smug and smirky. Linus kept grinning at him. Pure at least had the decency to act normal because the man was the only normal one in the bunch.

Gage was dressed in his finest suit, but the bastard was barely holding in his laughter.

"Break any more beds lately?" Gage asked without looking up from the file folder in front of him.

"It was one fucking bed, and dammit, it was old." Things had gotten a little too energetic the night they'd left the bed and breakfast. Now everyone fucking knew, and he wasn't living that shit down.

Eric, Ellison and him found it funny when it happened after a few minutes of shock. He was there with

Ellison on his cock and the mattress suddenly on the floor. Just because he found it funny didn't mean he wanted everyone else to know.

"Break a hip, you know—"

"I'd arrest your ass if I didn't need you, Linus."

"No, you wouldn't. I'm like your best friend."

"That doesn't say much about my sad existence. Can we get to work now?"

"We've been working, you've been counting and trying not to murder us since you got here," Raul stated from his spot beside Pure at the conference table.

"I don't think anyone needs to know about my sex life, that's between me and my boys."

"Did you forget who your friends are?"

"You're not my friends. You're annoying people I can't get rid of."

"We're fucking hurt, but not as hurt as your boys' asses if you broke the bed pounding one out. Nice one, man." Little snorted, then chugged an energy drink.

That kid didn't need caffeine. "Quit thinking about my boys' asses. What is it with y'all and your obsession with sex?"

"Aw, come on, man, most of us except Linus ain't getting any. We live vicariously through the erotic exploits of our friends."

"We're getting plenty, Little. We don't scare, well, except Pure he's—"

Raul cut Liv off with a growl, "Can we get back to fucking work?"

Raul's obsession with the innocent Pure was weird. The man wasn't going to do shit about it, but anyone made one comment about Pure, and the man went homicidal. The man needed to man up or just fucking let it go.

"Since Pure's boyfriend is ruining our fun…" Linus appeared disgusted by their ruined fun. "Little, what have you found out?"

"Shipments—"

"People," Gage corrected.

"*People* are being shipped about once a month, been no sign of activity the last three weeks. The reports that I've found and what Hunter came up with, there're sightings last Sunday of every month. Kinda weird if you ask me. A venture as profitable as what they have going on. Shit, the numbers are staggering."

"Hunter said that it's a small operation based out of Atlanta and New Orleans. Seems when Thorpe went down, his partners scaled back, possibly to cover their asses. The names in the files are the main players that we could find. There're several dirty cops on the payroll. From small-town deputies to state police." Gage pointed to the flat screen TV. "I talked to King."

"What did he have to say about it?" he asked as he studied the faces on screen. A few he recognized from his days with the state police. No one he'd worked with directly but that didn't mean anything.

"Same as when we were dealing with Thorpe. Truckers make extra cash with shipments. Weights are fucked with to make it passed weigh stations. Sometimes they pick up runaways, contact someone and turn them over for a hefty fee. Enough coordination and the same Troopers are on duty, and they wave the identified transport through."

Linus sat on the long table in front of the window. He observed as the man lost the amusement of minutes before.

"What you thinking, Linus?"

"Pelter, I'm thinking these people fucked up when they thought to use Powers. But with this amount of corruption? It has to go a lot higher than some Troopers. Did anyone hit your radar?"

He nodded to Gage and the man pulled up the pictures he'd emailed him earlier.

"This was my team, most good guys, a lot with ex-wives or kids in college. They pocketed cash but left the drugs. Not enough evidence to indict. There was one guy, in particular, I had my eyes on. But the problem was, I couldn't take it higher up the command." He walked toward the screen and pointed at the bastard in particular. "He disappeared quite a bit during our operation here to take Thorpe down. He's closeted, so I thought he was just meeting a trick while out of his territory."

"What makes you suspect him?" Liv drew his attention.

"He worked on the Louisiana State Police. Why he left was a mystery. Just one day he was transferred into my unit. He didn't meet the profile. Most of the guys I worked with worked their way up. I wasn't given a choice about his assignment. For a while, I thought he was a plant, since I already suspected some of my team of being dirty. I couldn't go to anyone, so I contacted a friend at the FBI. I trusted him."

"What he have to say?"

"Gage, it was the same bullshit. The amount of human traffickers is fucking ridiculous. They deal in runaways. Women smuggled in from other countries who have no one who's going to miss them. We don't find out shit until we find bodies or we luck into finding where they're being shipped in from. Gallen took a lot of personal time on the clock. I had my friend check his financials. Nothing seemed odd. Which didn't surprise me."

"Dirty cops stay hidden so fucking long because they know what not to do unless they get greedy. But with your former team—"

"We were trained to find the clues. Yeah, Liv, I tried my damnedest to find out who was who and all I had was speculation and no real evidence. Except for one thing, a witness. She wasn't going to talk and sure as fuck wasn't going to stand up in court and point him out. She went off grid about two months before I moved here.

"I thought with me gone, they'd slip up, but again nothing. They froze me out. When I got the reports of activity out at Thorpe's place, I went out a few times. Always missed whoever it was, but fresh tracks meant someone was out there. It's out of the way."

"Yeah, in this town, you gotta know the spots. Thorpe's place, even the kids don't go out there to drink or party." Little stood and grabbed another energy drink from the fridge.

"How do you not have a heart attack?"

"It's the only thing that keeps me going." Little took the spot beside Linus. "I had a friend hack into aerial photos, maybe track down times. The best I can tell, its monthly. Quick in and out trips, off-load the merchandise and head out again. Next weigh station they pull out the correct paperwork with the right info. Free and clear."

He tugged at his goatee in frustration. "If it is Gallen, then he knows this is my town."

"He thinks you're getting too close and he's going after yours."

He didn't need Linus to point out his greatest fear. He wasn't stupid enough to think that Gallen hadn't done his homework.

"That's the biggest worry I got right now. Eric and Ellison are staying out at my place. I don't know. I don't want to freak them out, but—"

"You don't got a choice, man. We'll set up a guard," Livingston offered.

"Me and Raul can split the shifts. When Pelter's with them they're good," Pure spoke up. "Besides, Sin and Saint know us, and they'll be more comfortable instead of bringing in outside contractors. I could call some of my old teammates who owe me a favor or two, but strangers in town draw attention."

"Yeah, I'll go home tonight and talk to them."

"We'll set up a rotating watch. Wren wouldn't mind pitching in when he's not on duty. My team is single, most of us don't have a family to target. I'll meet with the Crews and tell them to keep an eye out. The partners are pretty observant, and they rarely go anywhere alone. We're a pretty paranoid group." Linus poured himself another cup of coffee.

"Man, if I brought this shit to y'all doorsteps—"

Linus cursed and shook his head. "Pelter, this ain't your fault. Thorpe set this place up with his years of running dirty out at his place. We set an example. You might not think you made much of an impact around here, but this place is hundred times better with you protecting this town. We sure as fuck don't want to go back."

"We'll take care of this. I got the PR covered, and Peaches will handle any unpleasantness of possible jail time." Gage leaned back in his chair.

He knew Linus was right, but it didn't help the fact he felt guilty. He'd possibly put his boys in danger, and that was something he couldn't accept.

"I better get going, Layla's out at my place with Eric and Ellison."

"Meeting the future mother-in-law."

"Don't sound so fucking amused, Linus. I've never met parents before."

"About fucking time, and don't even think about having anyone perform the ceremony or Lily will kill you."

"Who said anything about marriage?"

"You know you're marrying those boys of yours. I'm just surprised you didn't do it after the first night they stayed at your place."

"Shut up, Linus, I have to survive meeting their mom, and then I'll think about rings."

"Whatever you say. We got this handled. I'll call when we set up mission planning."

"Thanks, Linus, everyone. I hate that I brought this here."

"Ain't your fault, don't know how many times gotta tell you that. I'll have Hunter take care of a few things."

"I don't want to know."

"I wasn't going to tell you."

"I'm already so far off the books with this one."

"You're Sheriff around here. Your operation. As long as it's on your book, doesn't matter. Your investigation, your rules."

They took care of a few more details and then he left, not feeling much lighter. As the weeks passed and his investigation stalled, he hadn't had a choice but to contact Linus. The situation had to end, and he didn't want to deal with the bullshit. He was ready for a nice, quiet life with his boys and this situation was fucking with his plans. If it was Gallen, that fucker would regret being anywhere near Eric and Ellison. His family came first, and their safety was the only thing that mattered to him.

16 They Didn't Need a Security Detail

His body was pleasantly sore after a quickie before his mama arrived from shopping in town. Yet what ruined him and Saint's post-orgasmic bliss was the fact Camden wanted them to have security. He understood it and knew how shit was when Thorpe ran the town, but they didn't want to account for their every move—at least not to anyone besides Camden.

Their man made them promise though, and what Daddy wanted, Daddy got. Why he loved that annoying man, he didn't know. Okay, he did, Pelter was damn near perfect. He took care of them. Their every need was met. They were always safe, and they couldn't take that away from Camden. They didn't need a security detail though. They were capable of taking care of themselves.

"Eric, are you dressed," his mama yelled through the door.

"Yes, but when has that stopped you?"

He laughed as the door opened. His mama hadn't changed much since the last time they saw her. She was thin, but her muscles were defined by the work she did.

"Where's your man at? He isn't hiding, is he?"

"No, Camden isn't hiding. He had a work call, and I think he went to his office. Saint was with him."

"We're not going to walk—"

"If you were twenty minutes earlier then you would've walked in on something."

She linked her arm with his, and they walked downstairs. He slid the doors of Camden's office open. Saint was perched on Camden's desk, Camden's arm lay across his lap, and Camden was just hanging up.

Camden stood up but leaned down to kiss Saint before striding around the desk and extending his hand toward Mama. "Sorry, Linus needed some information. Mrs.—"

"Please, call me Layla."

"Layla, I'm Camden, it's a pleasure to finally meet you. Ellison and Eric have told me a lot about you."

"I've heard a lot about you too, over the years. Was surprised when they told me you'd agreed to date them."

He tensed waiting for the awkwardness. Camden just grinned and wrapped his arm around Saint as his twin leaned into Camden's side. It was a silent show of support. Their man had told them he was nervous about meeting their mama and they didn't blame him. Camden hadn't dealt with parents or a long-term relationship before.

"I have to be honest, I'm pretty stuck in my ways, and my former job was a dangerous one. They met me when I was still working with the state police. Undercover work doesn't really allow for healthy relationships especially ones that haven't been established. I've made too many visits to loved ones left behind, and I didn't want that for someone."

"Sounds very lonely."

"It was. But when I moved here, I wanted something different, and my boys are beautiful and sweet. There was no way I could resist making them mine."

"You going to marry my sons?"

"Mama, that's not—"

"When the time is right, and they're sure they want to be tied to this old man permanently, I'll ask them."

He didn't know what to say, he stared at his brother and then they both turned their full attention to Camden. He'd said it like it was nothing, a done deal when they were ready. Oh shit, until he'd said it, they hadn't wanted to hope for more than they had with Camden, but now it was more.

"I would've rather talked to them about that in private, but I don't hide what they are to me in public so I sure as hell won't do it in our house. Before y'all came in, Ellison was telling me dinner was about ready. We can continue the interrogation over a meal."

"I'd like that, Camden." Layla just smiled and turned to leave the room.

"Don't gawk, I won't ask until we're all sure, but you two are mine. I know it's only been a few months, but to be honest, I didn't stand a chance of resisting. Even when I said no the night you two came up to me at Brawlers, it killed me to say it. Now, let's go eat, and your mom can ask me all the embarrassing questions she wants."

They nodded and accepted kisses, then he took their hands and led them to the kitchen.

"Boys, sit."

"Yes, sir," they answered and took their usual places. Saint on the right side of Camden's spot and him on the left.

They watched amused as their mama observed Camden make their plates and fill their glasses before he even thought about doing his own. Each was served which was followed by their forehead kiss. Dinner time was only second to bedtime. They were tucked in while Camden showered, and then they separated to allow Camden between them.

"Does he do this every night?"

"Yes, he likes to make sure we're fed before he makes his own plate."

"Layla, would you like—"

"No, I can make my own, but…thanks."

"Not a problem, but you go first." Camden motioned to the serving platters and bowls on the island.

"Mind if I ask a question?"

"I'm an open book, except for my past cases, those I don't talk about."

"Wouldn't ask about your work. Does your family know about my sons?"

"My parents aren't accepting even though I've been out longer than your sons have been alive."

"Then what brought you to Powers?"

They darted their glances at their mama and Camden.

"Boys, eat, you don't have to wait."

Camden didn't like the thought of them being hungry or tired. He wondered what their mama thought about Camden and the way he treated them. It couldn't be faulted. The man hadn't done anything but take care of them, even when they didn't know he was. After they'd started dating, they heard the stories about what Camden did before he'd showed his interest.

"I came here to stop my cousin and his crew from being taken out by the old Sheriff. He was racist and homophobic. After he was taken out, I went home. Back to my job. One night Peaches showed up and told me I was taking the Sheriff's job, and she wasn't taking no for an answer."

"I always did love Peaches," Layla said as she finished filling her plate and carried it to the table.

"At first, I did say no, but then I thought about it. A new life. Probably simpler with a chance at something different."

"Did Eric and Ellison play a part in your decision?"

Camden filled his glass with iced tea and then took his seat with his plate.

"Maybe unconsciously. I swore I was too old for them, but the longer I was around them—" Camden looked at them. "The less I wanted to resist. I still don't understand what they see in me, but I'm lucky to have them. Please, eat."

"I didn't know if you—"

"We don't," Camden and they answered together.

"What are you doing for the holidays? It's coming up quick."

"I thought if they wanted they could decorate the house, but I planned on spending it with them. Still got a few months to plan though. Last year I had all the crews out here. My place is the only one big enough for all of us. You're invited. You were on a trip I think last year."

"I'm always on trips. Busy keeps me from thinking too much. Me and their father didn't have very many holidays together. I tend to like to spend the holidays alone since my kids found a family to spend it with."

"Well, like I said, you're invited."

"Thanks, I'll think about it."

"No pressure. I think Powers has the largest number of atheists for a town this size. We don't do much but eat and hang out. Presents for the kids at Christmas."

"Do you think about kids?"

"I used to."

"Mama." Saint glared at her.

"I was just asking."

"It's fine, baby. I don't mind the questions. I'm forty-five. I think my having a family days' passed a long time ago."

He studied Camden again as they silently seemed to agree to start eating. The man's mood had changed, and he wasn't as relaxed as he'd been. They'd never brought up the kids conversation. It wasn't that they didn't want kids, Saint had always talked about having maybe one if they ever met someone who'd agree to it. He wondered if Camden had given up the thought of a family at the same time he'd decided relationships didn't mesh with his line of work.

Another one of those selfless things where Camden thought about everyone but himself especially children that hadn't even been thought about.

"Eric, I'm fine, I can see your brain working. Eat your dinner. Nothing is wrong."

"Okay."

He agreed but didn't believe him. It was there in his pale green eyes and the stiff set of his shoulders. They'd talk about it later when their mama wasn't there. The conversation that followed was lighter. About the trips their mama had coming up. How work was going for them. Stories about the crews and catching their mama up with the latest gossip. It was fun with no pressure. Still, their mama might not notice, but when he met Saint's gaze, he knew his twin noticed it too. They'd make everything right—it was what Camden deserved.

17 Their Future

As much as he loved his mama, it was nice to have the house back to just the three of them. Sin was stripping the bed in the room their mama used, and he was cleaning the kitchen from lunch. Camden hadn't been around a lot. Whatever was going on was serious, and since they'd have to deal with a partner in law enforcement, they'd have to get used to the hours. They'd gotten a taste of it. They hadn't slept without Camden, but it also gave him and Sin time to themselves.

Camden left a few hours before, but he'd called to say he was on his way home.

"Are we going to talk to him?"

He almost asked Sin what he was talking about but knew it wouldn't work. They'd whispered about it a few nights waiting for Camden to come home from work.

"Maybe he doesn't want to do it, Sin?"

He didn't want to pressure Camden into anything. He turned away from the sink and grabbed a towel to dry his hands.

"We'll never know if we don't ask."

"Just because I've always wanted kids doesn't mean–"

"You're letting your doubts take over and what's our Daddy's rule?"

He grinned at the Daddy's rule question. That wasn't used much outside sex but— "I can't believe—"

"You like calling him Daddy, so I don't even want to hear it. So, are we going to ask?"

"Yes, but if it makes him sad, I'm blaming you." He couldn't get over how Camden seemed to withdraw when the subjects of kids came up. It seemed to be a touchy subject. He and Sin agreed that Camden was too selfless. He thought about the impact it would have on others just like when he hadn't wanted to date or fall in love when he worked undercover. But that wasn't Camden's life any longer. He wouldn't say Camden's job was safer just different.

"Deal and Lou said she'd do one more surrogacy if we asked her."

"But I want Camden to donate. Can you imagine our daughter?"

He'd started to secretly imagine a daughter with Camden's green eyes, but knew their daughter would probably come out with blue eyes like Lou.

"Why a daughter, why not a son?"

"I'd be happy with whatever, but I'd kinda like a little girl. Ricky is so beautiful, and since they'll biologically be half-siblings, I kinda imagine, ya know?"

"But Peace is cute too."

He couldn't deny the little ginger-haired boy was adorable.

"Yeah, but if he doesn't say yes, then it's kinda pointless to hope right."

"Then just ask him."

"Ask me what?" Camden strolled into the kitchen removing his belt and holster. "Did Layla get going okay?" Camden embraced them both and held them close to his sides.

"She left about an hour ago. We were just straightening up." Sin laced their fingers behind Camden's back.

He silently took his brother's offer of support. They'd agreed to share a partner and that one day he'd want kids. Sin even said he'd love being a dad, but they'd have to find their man first. That's what they'd done, and it was time to ask if Camden would be open to one day doing it.

"So, what did you want to ask?"

"Um, well, I was just, you know—"

"Ellison, there's no need to be nervous. I can't take care of what's bothering you if you don't tell me."

He couldn't resist when Camden got that soft look in his eyes. The one focused on him or Sin when they were unsure. Camden always wanted them to be honest with him about everything so that he could make it better. "It's about what Mama asked the first night she was here. Did you ever want kids?"

"Let's put it like this. Do you want kids, Ellison?"

"I always thought one day, but if you don't want them, then that's fine."

"How would we have said kids?"

"It would only be one. Lou only agreed to act as surrogate one more time, but only for me."

"So, this is something you've already discussed with Lou?"

"Not recently, it was on one of our Saturday night sleepovers."

"Have a seat at the table."

He felt his shoulders slump as he released Sin's hand and took his usual seat. He laced his fingers together as he avoided glancing at Camden. He didn't want to see the sadness or that stiff posture he'd noticed the other night.

"What did you discuss with Lou? And when you talk to me you look at me."

He obeyed. "Just that if we ever met someone...that she'd act as a surrogate. She's done it for Lucky and Priest, Ghost and Harper."

"Who would donate, you?"

"Well, I wanted you to."

"Do you think we're ready for kids?"

"We don't have to do it yet. I just thought if we ever got to that point, you'd like to have a daughter with us."

"He's obsessed with the daughter thing."

"Sin, I said I'd be happy with whatever, but our daughter would be gorgeous and strong. Capable. I could teach her to fly, and you could take her skydiving or base-jumping the first time. We could take her mountain climbing and teach her how to rappel at a run down the side of a cliff face."

"A boy can learn those things too."

"I know, Camden." He'd just been dreaming of a little girl with black hair and deeply tanned skin. One that looked a lot like Camden. She'd be tall and strong. They'd raise her to be confident and independent. She'd never want for anything and Camden would always make sure she was safe.

"First, you two would have to marry me and then we'd decide on the kid thing when we were all ready."

His heart picked up inside his chest. Painfully beating against his ribs at Camden saying they'd have to marry him first. So what it had only been a matter of months they'd been dating, but they'd known each other for two years. He knew what kind of man Camden was, and if he took care of them so well before they married, he knew it would be stronger afterward.

"We're ready, Saint's been ready forever, so it would just be when you're ready to put that donation in a little cup and get our baby mama pregnant."

"So is that a possible yes?"

"It's not a possible yes, it is a yes, but not until we've had some more us time. I've been around long enough to know the crew kids are a top priority, and I'd like to make you two that for a while. Okay?"

"Okay." It was a yes, and he could live with that. He'd text Lou to reserve womb space for one at a later date. Lucky's sister never wanted kids of her own, but she'd talked about how happy seeing Lucky and Priest with Matty made her. Lou dealt with her own demons and kept a lot of secrets. But as much as Lou wanted everyone to think she was cold, she was loving and kind. Lou just didn't know how to express it.

"Don't you two have a gig at Brawlers this weekend?"

"Yes, it's been a while. Since Melanie graduated, King and Linc decided to take their honeymoon. Mama set them up with a month-long cruise. She called in a few favors she'd held on to. Melanie's looking forward to having Mal to herself for a whole month."

"It'll be good for King and Linc to have some time alone."

"So one more gig before they leave. You coming to watch us?"

"I wouldn't miss it and this time around I can dance with my boys like I wanted to."

He relaxed muscles he hadn't known were tensed. Camden did so much for them without asking for anything in return. Camden still made sure he gave them each equal attention. The sex was amazing, and sometimes it was nothing more than Camden getting them off and him not taking for himself.

"Ellison, I know you're nervous about talking with me sometimes, but I really want you to understand that nothing you ask will ever make me mad. You and Eric being happy is all I care about."

"What about you being happy?"

"Making you two happy makes me happy. If you two feel safe and content, then I've done my job. Not everything is going to be perfect. We're going to argue and disagree, but as long as we're open and honest about what's bothering us, then it can be fixed. I love you both and part of loving you is making sure you're okay. You need to trust me that I can take care of y'all."

"We do." He and Sin got up and found their way onto Camden's lap. They wrapped themselves around him. "We love you too."

"Good. Now, how about we go to bed. You two don't have to be quiet now. I miss you two screaming my name."

"Yes, Daddy."

They jumped up, and a smack landed on his ass as they took off for the steps. "I expect you two naked and ready for me, hands and knees."

"Yes, sir."

"How bad do we have to be to get a spanking?" he asked Sin.

"What did we do last time?"

"I think we weren't naked and ready."

"How slow do you think we can walk?"

They giggled as they slowed down and took their time getting to the bedroom. He knew Camden liked to see them naked when he came to their bed. Camden also loved to see the marks he left. The bruised impressions of his teeth. The fingertip bruises on their hips and the handprints on their asses. That's why he always wanted them waiting on their hands and knees. Camden gave them so much and asked for so little, so when he asked, they gave. It was the least they could do for the man they loved and who loved them back.

18 When Did His Life Turn Into A Freak Show?

There's a very short list of things that would scar him for life. Walking in on his parents having sex: never happened. Having to sit in a van with a stoned Little for two days: happened more than once. And now he could add walking in on Scary fucking Tank while Elijah jerked off to that list. He was sitting at the bar trying to drink that vision away waiting for his cousin and his men to finish whatever they were doing. Because the three men barely paused when he opened the fucking door.

"Eye bleach, my friend, eye bleach," Twitch whispered as he poured him another double.

"I may need therapy." He downed the double and tapped his glass on the bar top.

"No, you'll need therapy when you walk in on double penetration. How Elijah takes those two, he must live with a plug in."

"Twitch?" He looked at Twitch.

"What?"

"Never mention Elijah with a butt plug so he can take my cousin's dick ever again."

"You're such a prude, it's shameful."

"I'm not a prude."

"Whatever you say. You know, it's probably not a good idea to get drunk in your uniform."

"I'm off duty, but fuck, you're probably right." He slid the drink away to the rail and sighed as he scrubbed his hands over his face.

"So, what made you desperate enough to come see Scary?"

"He's family."

"Want to mend those childhood rifts?"

"Well, it seems like he's all the family I got."

He tried to ignore the phone call he'd made to his mother earlier, but it just kept coming back to him. Part of him thought if he'd told her that he'd found his happy ever after that she'd maybe be at least a little happy for him. It wasn't like she hadn't known. He wasn't going to hide what he felt for Ellison and Eric, or that one day he'd marry them. Lily would perform the ceremony. Even though they were already pretty much living with him, he hadn't asked them to give up their place. He still wanted them to have freedom.

"Did you take notes?" Scary's amused voice made him groan.

He didn't want to turn around. He'd never be able to look at them again.

"Drinking on the job, Sheriff, it couldn't have been that bad. My men are sexy together."

He shot a glare at Elijah. He'd heard the stories of the straight-laced and proper Elijah before he'd married Scary and Tank. They'd corrupted the beautiful man and Elijah didn't seem to mind.

"He's my cousin and—"

"Relax, walking in on someone is inevitable. Crave and Twitch like the women's restroom on breaks a bit too much."

"Thanks, doesn't make me feel much better, Elijah."

"Wasn't meant to. Alright, Scary, Tank, don't forget Juvie's first show is tonight at eight."

"Would we forget our daughter's first gallery show?" Scary asked.

He watched Scary and Tank say goodbye to their man. They were so in sync with each other. Touches and kisses were equal—the love between them unconditional. It still shocked him to see his beast of a cousin that gone over someone. Scary had sworn relationships weren't for him. Maybe it was just Elijah and Tank. He'd felt Scary's love for Tank was hidden for decades. He'd noticed things back then but hadn't thought too much about it until he'd found out Scary had married Tank and Elijah.

Elijah left, and Scary turned to him. "These visits are becoming too frequent. What we fucking do now?"

"Nothing, besides if y'all did, Peaches would get you off free and clear with minimal effort."

"True. So, what's up?"

Tank took a seat, and Scary sat beside him. Tank didn't interact with him much, but that was old wounds. He didn't think the man still forgave him for locking Scary up. Twitch set the two men up with pints.

"I don't know, just got off the phone with Mother."

"Pleasant shit I'm sure."

His mother and father turned their backs any time Scary came into a room when they were kids. Their disdain for Scary's mother transferred to Scary. His parents hadn't even attended the funeral. He'd gone, but Scary didn't let him close. Yet he'd stayed at a distance as he watched the big man grieve with Tank beside Scary.

"I told her about Eric and Ellison."

Scary snorted and took a sip of the pint. "I bet that made her go into an undignified meltdown."

"You could say that. She uninvited me for the holidays."

"I'm sure that hurt your feelings."

"Not so much. I didn't want to go anyway. She wasn't going to let me bring a date."

"Unless said date had tits and a pussy, no fucking way she would've let them through the door."

"Can't help it stings a bit though."

"Of course it does. Mama knew about me, said I needed to find a nice man, even grandma said the same. I don't know how your dad and my mama came from the same woman."

"I told Eric and Ellison I was going to talk to my mother about maybe—"

"They'll understand. Besides you got enough fucking family just from the Crews. It'll be all fucking good. Lily and Peaches for all their fucked-up quirks are the best mother figures most of us could get."

"Yeah, that, I've had to learn to ignore a lot of shit with y'all since I took over as Sheriff."

"We're a little fucked-up. Not everything we do is all that legal, but smoking a little weed every now and again, maybe making a few bodies—"

"No, I don't want to know about disappearing bodies."

"Prude," Twitch whispered, and he shot the little man a glare.

"I'm not a prude. I'm just…things are so fucking different here. I go from living by the book, no deviations and now, I don't know."

"You got a helluva fucking gig, man. Not to mention two young men that love your old ass. You don't need your parents bullshit."

"I just don't—"

"I know what you don't want to do, but your parents being dicks ain't got shit to do with what you got with Sin and Saint."

"I'm going to marry them at Christmas." He hadn't said that aloud. When they'd talked about having kids, all that shit he'd put to the back of his mind—the things he knew he couldn't have—came back to him. He hadn't lied to them when he said he wanted to one day, but one day in the near future. And the look on Ellison's beautiful face when he talked about a daughter. He wanted that happiness to come true for them. He'd already had a private talk with Lou, but he told her to keep it quiet.

"Okay, wait the fuck up, info like this would've spread like the plague."

"I ain't asked yet. I got them rings today on my lunch break."

"Well, Camden Pelter hardass extraordinaire has met his matches."

"I'd like for you to be best man."

"What, me, I don't—"

"Come on, Scary, you're the only blood family I got left, and we might not get along or really like each other all that much, but I'd really like my family there."

"Then I'll be there. Lily and Peaches will lose their shit when they find out they get to plan another wedding."

"I'd complain, but Lily and Peaches plan amazing weddings...and kidnappings."

"We all have our talents. Speaking of talents, Juvie is going to be looking for us."

Tank and Scary stood, and he could see the pride they had for their daughter. Juvie was twenty and making a go of it with metal sculptures. He'd noticed a pattern when it came to the crew kids—they were encouraged to do their own thing. No limits were set on what they could do.

"How's the art thing working for her?"

"She loves it, and it keeps her semi-out of trouble. Unfortunately, she's not a juvenile anymore, so we got that bail fund started."

They headed for the door together, and he caught the door Tank held open for him, then Tank took off for their bikes.

"She's a good kid."

"Yeah, she is, she's still working through some shit, but it is what it is. She didn't have the best start."

"Go, I have to head home, but my boys might not be there. I'm sure they wouldn't miss a crew kid's special day. Tank still hasn't forgiven me."

"That's never going to happen. Tank has a long memory. You locked me up, but also let that fucker who tried to kill him go."

"I didn't have—"

"It'll work out. Now, go home to your men."

He waved Scary and Tank off. He had a lot of regrets, but he'd been great at his job. Since moving there though, it didn't seem as important. That didn't bode well for his continued job as Sheriff. The town was different. He didn't look the other way like Thorpe had. Yeah, he let a few things go here and there, but he fought his battles where he could. He'd gone head to head with Peaches too many times and come out the loser.

He strode across the lot to his Sheriff-issued vehicle and started his short trip home. He was going to ask his boys to marry him. It wasn't going to be fancy and probably not all that romantic, but he only had a few more months until Christmas. Not a lot of time to get everything planned. He wondered if he was crazy for doing this since they hadn't dated more than four months. He wouldn't deny it felt right and he sure as hell wasn't going to pass up the opportunity to have what he'd always wanted. So many years he'd denied what he'd dreamed of having, and he wasn't going to do that anymore. Yes, Eric and Ellison would always come first, his priority, and if they were able to add to their family, then that would be great too.

It was all coming together. He just hoped nothing came along to fuck it up. He'd waited too fucking long for this, and the time he'd wasted denying himself and his boys—no time for regrets. All that was left was to put his plan into action. He smiled as his brightly lit house came into view. Both his SUV and the boys' car were parked out front.

This is what he'd been waiting for. It wasn't about anything other than waiting for Eric and Ellison. This was right and worth any risk. If he only had a year or fifty with them, he'd fucking cherish each one. Now, to ask his boys to marry him.

When he rushed inside, he heard Eric and Ellison's voices coming from the kitchen. Their soft laughter filled his house. He removed his belt, stowed his service weapon in his office safe, and made his way to the kitchen. He stopped in the doorway. Eric and Ellison were working at the stove. The table was already set.

"He'll be home soon."

"Daddy won't be mad if dinner isn't ready as soon as he walks in the door." Eric bumped Ellison with his hip.

"I know, but he always has dinner ready when we get home. This doesn't look like the picture on the recipe. What did we do wrong?"

"Nothing's wrong. All those pictures are professionally taken. It'll taste fine. Now, who's going to make dinner late?"

"Daddy makes this look so easy."

Ellison was getting better, but his baby had moments of insecurity still. He'd have to work harder to make Ellison more secure. He cleared his throat the minute he saw Ellison's shoulders drop and he seemed to pull into himself.

"Something smells good."

"It's—"

"Ellison."

"Thank you."

"That's better." He reached into his pocket and pulled out the tiny bag that held the two rings. "Come here. I have presents for you two."

"Presents!" Eric grabbed Ellison's hand.

Once they stopped in front of him, he took a deep breath and dropped to his knees. "Now, I know we talked about waiting until all three of us were ready, but I love you two, and I want to know if you'd like a Christmas wedding?"

He observed their expressions as they shifted from shock, to confusion, and then huge, bright smiles spread across their full lips.

"Yes," they both squealed.

He stood as they held out their left hands and he slipped the simple white gold bands on their fingers. He pulled the other bag out and handed it to them.

"Your turn."

They both took the matching ring and together they slid it on. Eric and Ellison jumped and threw themselves against his chest, he barely caught them and then hugged them tight as he carried them into the kitchen.

He whispered as he kissed Ellison's neck then Eric's, "Lou will be expecting our call in January. Let's have dinner and celebrate."

They didn't say anything, only nodded, and never loosened their hold on him. He wasn't ready to put them down yet, soon, but not yet. The night wasn't about the job to come or the dangerousness of it, it was all about his boys, and they said yes to marrying a cranky, old Sheriff.

19 Oh, Shit, They Were Getting Married

It still hadn't sunk in, Camden had asked them to marry him. On his knees and rings, they hadn't expected it and were shocked. He still kept looking at the ring, Camden said they could pick another one to exchange during the ceremony, but he wanted the one he had. It was perfect, and it meant they belonged to Camden. Not only were they getting married they were going to have a baby too.

"You've had that sappy grin on your face all day," Sin said as the other man leaned on the counter.

"Because he wants to marry us."

"Of course he does, he said he did when he met Mama."

"Yeah, but this is a ring, and we already have a date."

He knew he probably looked silly; he didn't care, though. He finished out the deposit. Camden said that morning he had something he needed to take care of and wouldn't be home until late. That usually meant they'd already be in bed before he came in, so they'd decided to start packing up the house. Most of their stuff was thrift store finds they'd refurbished or repurposed. Broke and starting out meant you got creative.

"Still going to start packing tonight?"

"We'll get some takeout and some beer, drive Mrs. Bremerton mad one last time."

"Sounds like a plan."

He handed the bank bag to Sin, and his twin walked off to lock it in the safe. They had the day off tomorrow. Maybe they'd have Camden come to their house for the night. Camden had promised to borrow Little's van to help move boxes. Camden made them promise him that they make the house theirs. They could decorate however they wanted, but they liked Camden's place. Although it did need a few more personal touches, they had plenty of those at their house.

"Do you think Camden will mind us setting up stained-glass windows?"

"He said we could make whatever changes we want. There's that group of trees not far from the house. Down near the old gazebo. They'd be beautiful hung up around that."

"Yes, they would. You ready?"

"Almost I just have to—" The door opened. "Sorry, we're closed."

"Sin, Saint, we need to talk." The faint lines in Linus' face were deeper than normal, Liv, Pure, and Raul weren't looking any happier.

"What happened? This isn't a family—"

"We've been working an operation with Pelter. We lost contact with him a few hours ago, we received a message, and you two need to hear it."

He reached for Sin and held tight as Linus held out his phone.

"Linus, I'm down, shipment came in early." Camden's voice cracked, and it was laced with pain. "When you get this come with everything you got, but make sure my boys are safe. Tell them I love them. I'll hold these fuckers off—"

The call cut out.

"We can't pinpoint his location. Hunter's tried everything. We only know that he's somewhere within—"

"Was he wearing his watch when you met with him earlier?" Sin asked.

"Yeah, why? He said it was some—"

"Saint."

"On it." He pulled out his phone and pulled up the GPS locator. It was something they're mama had always done. He had a program that would tell him where Sin, his mama, and now Camden was. It was a habit they'd pick up working with Mama. Shit could go bad at any time on a climb. Mama had given Camden a matching watch as a present when she'd visited. He read out Camden's coordinates.

"We called in rescue, but if it's a standoff out there…"

"We're going in," he announced.

"No, Camden would have my ass."

"We don't give a fuck. That's our man out there. Give us Liv, Pure, and Raul, no one is more qualified to fly a rescue mission than us. We've been doing this for years. Either you help, or we'll do this our damn selves."

He stepped up beside Sin and dared Linus to challenge Sin.

"Listen, we've flown rescue missions in far more dangerous places than Powers. We know that area, and there's no team that could be out there quicker than me and Sin."

Fear was making him nauseous, but they'd done this. He'd flown in snow storms. They'd rappelled down sheer mountain faces to hook stranded climbers. They were more certified in being medics than half the EMTs in town. It was what they'd done.

"If this goes bad..."

"It won't, so, quit wasting our time and let us get to the airfield. You take care of what you need."

"I'll organize on the ground. I've called in favors. Get going, but you better be alive when this mission is done. I'm not dealing with your man."

"You won't have to."

They ran out with the other men behind them. Pure made a detour at Linus' SUV and pulled a case from the back. Linus was in the front seat, and as soon as Pure was clear, Linus sped off in the opposite direction.

Every detail played out in his mind. What they'd need. Scenarios that would make this a success or failure, but the latter wasn't an option. In the background, he heard Sin talking to Fred to tell him that he needed to come take care of closing down because they had an emergency.

The trip out of town seemed to take forever, and the airfield was another ten miles passed their place. He ignored the grumbling of the three big men in the back seat. They'd grown up doing this. They could work under pressure. They'd trained for it since Mama put them on their first climbing.

Camden had to be okay. They'd waited so long never with a true thought that months after Camden inviting them out to his place that they'd wear his ring.

"Saint, we got this. There isn't anything you can't do in the air, and I'm the most qualified to rappel in. All we have to do is remember what Mama taught us. We'll bring Camden home. I know it."

He nodded as they approached the turn-off. It was dark which hindered any rescue, but it wasn't impossible. They had the darkness to cover their approach. Ernie still had some night vision gear, cameras, and goggles. The nearest helicopter was black and big enough for all of them. It would be fine. He could do this. It was a fucking walk in the park. Because failure wasn't an option.

20 Camden Needed Them

They were out of the massive SUV before the others were even out of the backseat. He wasn't going to accept that fucked-up goodbye while his and Saint's man was in the middle of a fucking war zone.

"Ernie, is the new chopper fueled?" Saint yelled on the move.

Saint was off in the direction of their ride and was as calm as he was with any rescue they'd done, but he was sure this was eating Saint up as much as it was him. They'd have time to fall apart later.

"Serviced this morning. What's going down?"

"Rescue, we need a basket. I need the rappelling gear and chutes for at least four."

"Vests?"

"Yeah, you keep any of those smoke grenades around and masks?"

"How much cover are we talking?"

"I need enough time to rappel in, assess the damage and get Camden out. We got enough tree cover to keep Saint in the air."

"Free rappel from the chopper?"

"Fastest way to the ground. I need the night vision."

"I'm on it."

Ernie headed to the bunker for the gear they kept hidden.

"Sin, what the fuck is going on?" Livingston bellowed.

He didn't bother turning around to waste time and left Liv, Pure, Raul to follow if they wanted. This shit was second nature. When they couldn't wait for the authorities in the past, Sin and Saint were the first to organize a rescue. Their mother made sure they were prepared for anything.

"We locked on to the GPS in Camden's watch. We're monitoring his location. Saint will fly the rescue mission. The three of us will rappel in out of range of whatever weapons they have out there. Saint will circle and monitor with night vision and keep us informed from the air. You three badass, bounty hunter, ex-military will cover while I hook Camden in and get him in the air. Pure will act as sniper from the air and pull Camden in. Once he's secured, Pure can use the winch to get us out."

"Sin, what weight load are we talking?" Ernie appeared with bags slung over his shoulders.

"Camden is a good two-seventy, but I need enough to cover three hundred pounds to compensate for the basket."

"You're not going up with him?"

"I'll act as the belayer from the ground until we have him locked in."

He changed into his black jumpsuit and secured a matching parachute to his back.

"We ain't got all fucking day, gentlemen. Me and Saint will take care of this on our own if you ain't ready to be airborne in five minutes."

He was already on the move with Ernie and him double checking gear. Sin was doing a quick safety check.

"With night vision, I can go dark when we reach the drop zone." Saint snatched the black flight suit, slipped in on and finished his pre-flight check. "I checked the aerial photos of that area. There's a small clearing, not enough for a vehicle but safe enough to rappel in. He's about half a mile south of the DZ. Can you drag him that far? Because if you want to take the chance—"

"What's the rule, Saint?"

"Adrenaline is better than sex?"

"Not when it comes to Camden."

"Yeah."

"We got this big brother."

"Mama didn't raise cowards."

"Fucking right."

"Boys, I got the night vision camera, give me five to attach. Stay in constant contact. I'll be about a mile behind in case you have to bail out."

"Ernie—"

"Don't Ernie me, boys."

The Trenton Crew slipped on and secured their harnesses. He double-triple checked the equipment, carabiners, lines and everything else they needed. They got into the zone, and they were in the chopper as Saint readied for takeoff.

"Boys, what's the situation?"

For the first time in almost an hour, they smiled as they heard their mama's voice.

"Mama, our man is on the ground, unknown condition, and a tight drop zone," Saint answered.

He made sure everyone was in and secure, he strapped in and looked around at the three men staring at him and Saint like they'd lost their fucking minds. They might be big and fucking bad, but this was shit they were trained for.

"You're going to rappel in, and Sin, when your feet hit the fucking ground, you stay on the move. Smaller target and trust Saint to know how to get y'all out."

"Always, Mama."

"Good. Now, I'm patched in, so I'm there every step of the fucking way. We got this, boys. You were born and trained for this moment."

An instant calm came over him as they soared into the air. The vibration of the blades circling above them. In the air had been home for most of their lives. Saint was on Ernie's lap learning to fly before he could walk. He'd climbed before he took his first steps. There wasn't anything they couldn't do, and Mama had made sure they knew it.

"Gentlemen, you have fifteen minutes until drop. Check your weapons and egos. This is a rescue, not a takedown. We're in and out with as little fuss as possible. Don't fuck this up or you're going to regret it."

"Listen to my boys, or I'll make sure you're frozen on the side of a mountain, and they won't find your asses until thaw."

The lights went out, and he slipped his night vision goggles in front of his eyes. He tied the lines for Livingston, Raul, and himself, then he stood on the edge and took a breath. He threw the attached small chute to the basket and attached it to the line, then let it go.

"Bring him home, Sin."

"He'll be in our bed before sunrise. See you on the ground." Sin jumped face down, adrenaline instantly rushed through his veins, and he tightened his hold and slowed his descent as he closed in on the ground. Shots were loud on the ground.

"He's twenty feet to your right, Sin."

Two big bodies landed on either side of him, and he crouched as he made his way toward Camden's location. He stayed low as he noticed Camden hunkered down behind a tree. His heart nearly stopped as he saw his man was unconscious with at least two unfriendlies coming from the opposite direction. He didn't wait, he ran forward with the basket in his hand and pulled a pin on one of the smoke grenades. He sent it sailing as he fell to his knees. There was a flash, and he covered his nose and mouth with a bandanna.

He pulled compression bandages from his pockets. Camden groaned as he quickly went to work. Fuck, he was alone, and from what he could see, Liv and Raul were drawing fire. He slapped his hand over the emergency beacon.

"I got your location."

"What's the situation, son?" His mama's voice was strong and edged with steel. She stayed calm for them.

"Can't see much, but he's unconscious." He checked Camden's pulse. "His pulse is strong. The blood loss isn't dangerous yet, but I don't know if I'm missing wounds."

"We'll worry about that when we have him in the air."

It was a struggle to get Camden's big body maneuvered enough to get him on the board. He buckled him in and tightened the belts. He looked up as the wind picked up. A small flash signaled the ropes heading down. He grabbed them, clicked the carabiners on the steel hoops.

He wrapped the line around his back, securing the safety line.

"Start bringing him in, now."

Pure reeled Camden in, and seconds could've been minutes or hours. He could only see the slight outline of the basket. It was neon but the moonless night and thick cropping of trees hid its ascent.

"Package is secure."

He breathed out a relieved sigh.

"Drop the lines, Pure."

"Son, you're going to have to do this quick. Make yourself small."

"Raul, Liv, meet at the extraction point now."

"Go, get Camden out, we have backup coming. We can't leave these fuckers to get away."

He didn't argue with Liv. He grabbed the rope and locked in seconds before he flew from the ground. He did as his mama told him, he made himself small, and once he cleared the trees, Saint started to circle. Sparks flew as he used his ascender to pull himself up the wildly swinging rope and into the chopper. His muscles were on fire and he could barely catch his breath. He slipped his safety devices free and leaned between the seats.

"Fucker, we're hit."

He checked that Camden was still secured to the lines. He looked at Pure. The man nodded as he set his rifle aside and made quick work of getting Camden into a chute then strapping him back in. It wasn't perfect, but they weren't exactly in a place where they could complain.

"Can you set us down at a safe distance?"

"We're losing fuel and altitude."

"Get Camden back out, keep us moving enough for us to get Camden to the ground. Pure, you're going down with him. Keep him covered."

"You got it."

They didn't have time for goodbyes, or I love yous. Their man was unconscious anyway. The only thing they could do was hope they survived.

"Sin, I'm going to get us high enough to jump after we make sure Camden and Pure are on the ground."

"Boys, once you jump, you get your asses as far from the chopper as possible before deploying your chutes."

"Ready."

He held his breath as Pure and Camden went out. Pure would go down with him, far enough to pull the chute before his own.

"Ernie, you with us?"

"Turn on your lights, you two going tandem?"

"We'd have better maneuverability going solo especially with how far we need to get away from the chopper."

"Sin, hold on tight, I'm going to climb until we're at a safe distance to jump."

"Saint, once you reach a safe distance, you hit auto-pilot, and you two work fast. If you're losing fuel, you've got a tiny window."

Everything slowed as Saint took them into a steep climb and leveled out. Once Saint's hands were off the controls, they had to work quickly. Once Saint was out of the pilot seat, they reached for each other and stepped to the edge. Then they were in the air. He flattened his body and sailed away from the aircraft. The scent of smoke was thick, and he could see muzzle flashes below.

He deployed his chute, and the deceleration jarred his body. He couldn't see Saint, but he knew his brother was safe. An explosion brightened the area, and he saw Saint gathering his chute and running for the trees. He aimed for that direction and braced for impact. His body rolled, and he skidded to a stop. He was on his feet and running.

Pure's voice yelling his name had him jerking his gaze to the right and following the sound. Saint was already on the ground checking Camden over. Pure was standing guard with his weapon drawn.

"You two better be on the ground." Their mama's voice sounded in their earpieces.

"We are, and Ernie's going to kill us for crashing his new toy."

"Boys, as long as you're living, crash as many as you fucking want," Ernie's voice piped up. There was a bit of a crackle. "There's an area clear enough for me to come in for a landing about a mile from you. Going to try it or dig in and wait for reinforcements."

Pure answered for them, "I'd prefer to dig in, but I don't know Camden's condition. Which one of you has better aim?"

"Saint."

"You cover us, and I'll drag. I left rope tucked under Camden just in case."

"Let's do this. I'm on the ground in ten. I've got you covered once you get to the clearing. Don't tell the Sheriff…I'm kinda a felon."

Within minutes they were on the move, leaving the chaos and hell behind. He just hoped they did the right thing. They couldn't live without Camden.

21 Camden Arrested Every One of Them

"Sheriff Pelter, you need to remain calm. Do you remember what happened?" A baby-faced doctor hovered inches from his face.

Drugs muddled his mind, but he still hurt...everywhere. He panicked as he tried to remember what the hell was going on.

"No."

"You've received several injuries. We've removed three bullets, but we need to take you to the OR to remove a few we can't safely remove in the ER. Do you understand?"

"Yes, my boys, where are—"

"Camden, don't be a fucking idiot. Your boys are fine," Linus barked. *"Let them take the fucking bullets out."*

"I want to see them before I go." He wouldn't stand for them denying his demand to see them. Surgery meant serious damage, and he wasn't having it unless he could say goodbye to his boys first.

"We don't have time to waste. You've lost a lot—"

"Shut the fuck up and get me Eric and Ellison...now." He'd get up off this fucking bed if he needed to and he'd take anyone out who thought to stop him.

A large hand landed in the middle of his chest, and he looked up to find Gage glaring down at him. "We got this, man, I'll go get your boys." The understanding in the man's eyes caused him to relax. "Just do what the doctors want you to fucking do, got me?"

He nodded. He wasn't dying or at least he didn't think he was.

"Your boys flew a rescue mission to get your ass. They've finally crashed from the adrenaline and they ain't holding up that great," Liv remarked from by the door.

"What the fuck? Y'all were supposed—"

All the things that could've gone wrong played through his brain. He could've woken up only to find his boys had died. It highlighted all the time he'd wasted. The years he'd denied them and himself. His brain was fuzzy, and the pain ebbed away, but he fought it. He needed to see Eric and Ellison before they took him away. Tell them one more time he loved them and that they shouldn't have put their lives on the line for him.

The door opened, and he turned his heavy head to see them. His beautiful boys, tears stained their cheeks, and their eyes were red-rimmed. They held each other tight as if they'd fall apart without the tether to the other. His arm fell off the bed, and he tried to lift it to reach for them. It must have been all they needed because they ran across the room. They didn't touch him.

"Boys, what did you do?"

"We just did what had to be done. We couldn't lose you," Ellison's voice broke.

They took his hand in theirs, stroked their thumbs over his skin, and it was an instant relief.

"We were qualified."

"I don't give a shit if you were qualified or not. You put yourselves in danger, and you're going to be punished."

"It was worth it," they said in perfect sync.

He shook off their hold on his hand and fisted his fingers in their shirts. The thought of losing them was too much. That was why he'd stayed single all these years. He couldn't bear to put them through that. He had to protect them. His life wasn't meant for his boys. They'd be safer farther away from him.

"Sheriff, we really need—"

"Fuck off. One more fucking word, and I walk."

"Camden, please," Eric begged.

"You two go home."

"We don't want to go home without you."

"No, your house."

"Cam—"

"I'm ready to go. Linus, take them to get their stuff and take them home."

"This is bullshit, Camden. You don't want to do this."

"Just do what I fucking say," he growled as he released his boys and was thankful when he was wheeled out of the exam room. He wasn't strong enough to keep up the act. One look or tear, and he'd beg for forgiveness, but their safety came first.

Two weeks passed since he'd woke in the hospital while getting prepped for surgery surrounded by doctors, his deputies, and the Trenton Team.

The last thing he remembered was making the phone call to Linus to tell his boys he loved them. He'd never reacted with such fear in his life. The mere thought of never seeing his boys again or being their when their children were born killed him—there wasn't even the chance of kids yet. Since he'd sent them away, his house was cold and empty. He made excuses more often than not to avoid it as much as possible. He couldn't sleep in their bed anymore, and when he didn't catch a nap on his couch in his office, he curled up on a sleeping bag in his living room. His wounds weren't healing, and he wasn't getting enough rest, but in the short time they'd declared their relationship official, he'd grown used to things. The warmth of his boys tucked against his sides at night. The sight of them in his kitchen or on the couch when he got home from work. The calls and texts, he hungered for all those small incidences that made his life happy. He wanted to be happy because he'd been miserable so fucking long.

The anger and awe at what his boys had done hit him finally. He'd listened to the recordings Linus brought him. The man kept a record of his missions in case something went nuclear. Eric and Ellison had sounded so confident and strong. He'd known they were, but to hear it did something to him. Unfortunately, his anger kept them away. He couldn't get past the rage at the danger they put themselves in. He was supposed to protect them not the other way around.

He stood in the shadows across the street from Pleasure dressed in black.

Yes, he'd kept his boys away from him, but he couldn't resist his compulsion to make sure they were safe.

Peaches was on his ass to release the Trenton Crew from jail, but they were staying locked up as long he wanted. He'd arrested every member of the Trenton Crew for every suspected crime they'd committed. Peaches was earning her retainer.

"The stalker bullshit doesn't exactly work for you." He turned to find Bull leaned against a brick wall, his arms folded across his chest.

"What are you doing here?" he asked and went back to his watch.

"I drew the short straw. We couldn't send the Trenton Crew after you. I think they're all locked up except for Gage. Out of all of us, I was the least pissed off."

"Nothing you say will change my mind."

"I didn't say you needed to change your mind, but why not take your boys' feelings into consideration?"

"That's all I've been doing. They're the most important."

Why couldn't people see that what he did was to make sure they were always safe? He couldn't allow them to be in the same situation again. He wouldn't be able to survive it.

"Doesn't seem like it when you kicked them out of your room and house as soon as you woke up after they rescued your damn ass. Fuck, man, that shit they were trained for, and their mama trained them well. No one else could've pulled off a rescue like that as quickly as they did. You would've been dead before they flew a team in."

He stared across the expanse of the deserted street. It was almost time for his boys to get off work and go home. He'd make sure they got in their car before he returned to work.

"Don't fucking ignore me, man. You three love each other, anyone can fucking see it, but you're being a moron. How many fucking chances do we get? We're old. We're assholes. And our boys still love us. Do you think I didn't fight what I felt for Gregory? Do you fucking think for one minute I wanted him to be there when I decided being sober wasn't working? Gregory is a grown ass man, and I respected his decision, grateful every day he decided this old bastard was worth it. Don't give that shit up because of what might happen tomorrow or ten years from today. We ain't guaranteed a lot in life, Pelter. So when we get the chance, we hold onto the good to make the fucked-up in life less painful."

He understood what Bull was saying, and he may agree, but he—just the thought of leaving them to go on after him tore him apart. When he found out what they did, he was proud of their strength, but going on without them wasn't an option. They were…

"If you're thinking they'd be better off, you're wrong, man. They're falling the fuck apart. Maybe even more than you. In the three years Sin and Saint been coming around Brawlers ain't once in all that time have I never seen them without a smile on their faces. We used to believe that they couldn't survive without each other because they were made to be an inseparable set. Then you bring your fucking ass around, and those boys are broken—even together."

"They could've died. I just keep imagining waking up in the hospital and instead of them being there that Linus is telling me they didn't make it. I'd have to go the rest of my life knowing they died because of me. What happens—"

"Knock off the what-ifs. What if you have another fifty years with them or as little as a year. Would you rather not have that memory? Suffer with your fucking pride all you want, but don't take that shit out on them. They don't need your insecurities or be the victims of your martyrdom."

"This is my life, I chose it the day I enlisted, and when I pinned the badge to my uniform for the first time."

"A lot of military and law enforcement have great marriages despite the high divorce rate. If their spouses and partners go into it knowing that they gotta take hold of every day and make it great. You're going to end up a lonely, bitter man with nothing better to show for your life than a chest of metals. I'm not going to stand out here arguing with you all night. I got one thing to ask. Is their pain worth your ego?"

The man slapped him on the back, but he never turned to watch the man disappear. Would he survive walking away? Two weeks ago the answer was the same— he couldn't imagine life without them. He wanted his rings on their fingers, to see his boys hold their child for the first time, and celebrate every milestone. He checked the time and stepped out of the shadows of the alley. Even as his brain made the decision, his body and feet dragged with the terror of all the things that could go wrong. He hadn't bothered to think about the good things.

He hesitated with his hand on the door handle before the pulled it open. The obscene moaning over the PA system interrupted the music briefly. Once he was inside, he searched for Eric and Ellison, and they stared at him from the counter. Their expressions a mix of hope and misery; their fingers locked tightly together. They still wore his rings on their slender fingers. He'd noticed they looked skinnier—their faces thinner than the last time he'd seen them.

All his pain and loneliness threatened to double him in half. He'd missed them so much, and he didn't second-guess himself as he strode quickly toward them. He gathered them in his arms, they clutched at the back of his shirt, and he kissed them. Kissed their cheeks and wet lashes, and apoligized between each, he whispered he was sorry—begged for their forgiveness.

They were the only good thing he had in his life. The part that made it all worth it.

"We want to come home," their whispers were tearful, and they buried their faces against his chest.

"I'm so sorry. I just didn't...I could've lost you two, and it made me insane to know I wasn't there."

"Just take us home, please," Ellison begged, and that broke his heart.

Ellison needed him to be strong—be his safe place—and he'd let him down.

"Come on, finish up, and I'll take you home and make you dinner, how's that?"

They nodded, he let them go, but he didn't move away from them. He needed their closeness—the warmth of them. He'd make this up to them even if it took him the next lifetime to do so. He'd nearly broken his boys, and that couldn't happen again.

He told them he loved them, kissed their soft lips before he led them outside and toward work so he could pick up his SUV. He needed his boys home with him—now.

22 His Boys Were Amazing

White lights were stung through the trees around the gazebo in his side yard. The stained-glass window installation that had made its way to their house cast a colorful kaleidoscope of colors on the ground and gazebo. Lily and Peaches had outdone themselves decorating for their wedding.

It had been two months since the operation that had taken Gallen down. He'd been right about his old team, but he hadn't realized how deep and far it had gone. It was a group of twenty dirty cops. They'd saved nearly fifty young women and teenagers, but he knew that the problem wouldn't be solved, yet every rescue meant something. It also brought light to the issue no matter how people wanted to ignore it and say it wasn't a problem.

After he'd spent two weeks becoming a complete bastard to his boys, he begged their forgiveness.

His boys had earned a hell of a spanking after what they'd done. They endangered themselves, but in the course of it, they'd earned themselves new jobs to go along with the ones at Pleasure. They'd had to call in rescue choppers and personnel from bigger counties, but not anymore. His boys were the ones called in for rescues. He couldn't be prouder of them. They just weren't allowed in firefights anymore. They could jump from all the planes they wanted. They could fly to the moon and back, but going near gunfire was out.

"Hi, Camden." Layla stopped beside him.

"Hey, glad you could make it. You look beautiful." He couldn't get over the likeness of mother and sons. The same blond hair and delicate features. The only difference was Layla's dark brown eyes that appeared almost black, and Eric and Ellison had clear, pale blues ones.

"Camel ride and six transports, but I wouldn't miss my boys getting married for anything. I just wanted to say thank you."

"For what?"

"I've never been the greatest mother. They had more addresses before they were three than most people have in a lifetime. Yeah, I made their life fun, but it wasn't stable, and I know my sons craved something normal. You gave them that. You love them. It took you a while to realize it, but you did."

"I do love them. If you hadn't made them the young men they are, they sure as hell wouldn't have the skills to save me."

"I didn't say they weren't capable and a little addicted to adrenaline. When I lost their dad, he really was the love of my life, and I lost myself. I brought them up with a don't worry about tomorrow because it wasn't guaranteed attitude."

"I think that works for me. My job isn't the safest."

"Well, you know my sons can take care of you."

"And I'll take care of them."

"I'm going to go find them. It's almost show time."

She gave him a quick, awkward hug and hurried off toward the house.

"You ready for this, man? We can get you out of here fast," Liv asked from behind him, and he turned to find the entire Trenton Crew smirking at him.

"I'm not running. I got them, and I ain't giving them up."

"You got some great boys there. If they didn't belong to you, I'd be snatching them for myself. Beautiful and a little crazy, that's damn near perfect."

He didn't take offense. Liv avoided men at all costs. The man was severely scarred but still handsome, but the scars overshadowed his looks. Liv backed away when men came up to get a chance with the badass Trenton Team. He felt a bit sorry for him.

"I'll take that as a compliment."

"We just wanted to say good luck and congratulations." Gage held out his hand.

He shook it and looked at Little who was hiding something behind his back. It didn't seem the man realized he could smell it.

"Little, take a walk."

"Good deal, congrats, man." Little smirked and ran off, straight for Lily.

"We're going to go find our seats. I think Scary's waiting for you." Linus pointed passed his shoulder.

He turned his head to find Scary looking uncomfortable as fuck in a nice suit. He crossed the short expanse between them.

"Thank you for doing this, man."

"Don't thank me. To be honest, like you said a few months ago, we're the only blood we got. Look at them."

He let his gaze scan the yard and all the people seated or wandering around. Couples, triads, kids running around and babies in slings.

"This is what we got. Family is what we make it. It ain't always perfect. Some you want or may need to arrest, but we're here. Nothing says we have to be related by blood and they sure as shit don't require family to be normal. Here and now, you don't gotta be anything you ain't. You can be fucked-up, and we're still there when the phone rings."

"She didn't even return my calls after I sent the invite."

"This ain't about her or him. This is about you and your boys. None of that depressed shit today. Enough time for all that later, but again, these people in this yard, the ones that showed up…this is your family. Now game face, man, it's show time."

Scary pointed toward the house, and he looked up to find Eric and Ellison arm and arm with their mother. They wanted her to walk them down the aisle. Ernie was in the front row—the proud Dad position.

His boys were dressed in hippie style white linen shirts provided by Lucky and black jackets. Ellison had on a little extra makeup, and Eric had a new pink streak in his light blond hair. They were gorgeous. In the days leading up to the wedding, he'd lived in terror they'd come to their senses. It hadn't happened, and he'd gotten a call that morning making sure he hadn't changed his mind. That wasn't going to happen.

"You did good, Camden, really good," Lily whispered in his ear from behind him where she was positioned in the gazebo. The night was chilly, but they had heaters set up everywhere. There were just too many people to have performed the ceremony inside.

He held his hands out to Eric and Ellison. He tried not to notice that Layla held a little tighter before she let them go. He led them to stand at the base of the three steps, but never took his eyes off his boys.

"Before we start, Peaches and I want to take a minute to make an announcement. Camden, we're always honored when our boys come to us and tell us they found their person or persons. It's a parents' proudest moment to know that their kids found love and acceptance. No matter the shape, shade or gender, love is what we all want. And today, Peaches and I, get to witness the joining of you, Eric, and Ellison. Our boys have all found their persons. You've all given us daughters, sons, granddaughters, and grandsons. You've gifted us with miracles that no higher power could ever dream to bestow. Camden Pelter, you're a sometimes snobby, too lawful for your own good, asshole, but we love you and welcome to the family, son."

Lily and Peaches were on either side of him, their lips pressed against his cheeks, and he closed his eyes.

"You're accepted and loved. You were ours the minute you brought your oversized ass to us."

"Thank you both."

"Now that that bullshit is out of the way, let's get these three married because I need a smoke."

"Lily," he warned, and she smirked at him.

"You see nothing, Sheriff, remember that."

His boys chuckled, and he turned to look down at them. "I love you both, and I will do everything in my power to always make you happy."

"We know, you already do," Eric and Ellison spoke in unison.

Lily began the ceremony, even though it wouldn't be all legal. He and Ellison had the marriage license, but this would join him with them both. He didn't need some piece of paper to tell him they belonged to him and he was theirs. He'd waited a lifetime for a family of his own, his boys were that, but so were everyone else sitting in his yard. He'd come home when he'd accepted this job, and he'd found everything he wanted in a small Georgia town—far more than he expected.

Epilogue: Lou Was A Badass!

Oh, fuck, they'd done that to Lou, and she was going to kill them in their sleep. That was one of the nicest threats they'd received over the last twelve hours since she'd gone into labor. His boys had rubbed her legs, feet, back, and catered to her every need the past nine months. They'd even moved her into the house so that he and his boys wouldn't miss a kick or an appointment.

He was sorry she was about to push out a ten-pound baby. He'd already apologized so many times. He cringed as she let out another scream and a steady stream of curses followed. Lou stood beside the bed, rocking her hips from side to side.

"Lou, come on, you have to breathe." Carmen, the maternity nurse, smiled and spooned more ice chips between Lou's lips.

He kind of figured something might be going on between those two, but Lou grumbled and said they were only friends.

"I don't want to breathe and why didn't I get a fucking C-section?"

"Because if I remember correctly, someone wanted the fathers to experience the miracle of birth."

"Horror, horror of—"

Another scream cut off what she was going to say. He rushed to the bed as Dr. Hampton strolled in with a smile on his face.

"Are we about ready to push?"

"I'm ready for drugs." Lou collapsed onto her forearms on the bed, her dirty blonde hair stuck to her face.

"Let's get you checked…the baby is doing great."

As much as they wanted to know what they were having, they'd decided against it. Apparently, Lou knew but respected their wishes.

"Come on and lie down on the bed."

"Could you hold me, Camden?" Lou asked, looking miserable.

"Of course." He crawled onto the bed and leaned back, then helped Lou sit between his thighs. She rested against his chest.

He'd do anything for Lou. She was about to give them the best gift ever. He held her and massaged the sides of her belly. Eric and Ellison wrapped their hands around her knees as the doctor lifted her gown. His beautiful husbands watched Lou with such love and awe on their faces. They'd thanked Lou every day.

"Fully dilated, Lou, you know what that means."

"When I feel like pushing, push."

"You've done this before. You're a pro."

"You're a badass, Lou. You got this," he whispered in her ear and felt her small nod.

Suddenly, time was measured in heavy panting breaths, screams, and softly whispered encouragement from him and his boys. Minutes could've passed or hours, it didn't matter. Eric and Ellison held her legs as she pushed, he rubbed the tensed muscles of her stomach.

"Come on, Lou, I see black hair, you're almost there, on the next contraction bear down and push."

The time came, she curled her upper body forward and groaned through the longest push.

"Another one, the head is out."

He held his breath as she screamed, and then she collapsed. It seemed like forever before they heard the baby cry. He lifted his gaze to see a head of black hair as the doctor worked.

"Gentlemen, you have a gorgeous baby girl."

"Elisabeth, her name's Elisabeth." Ellison seemed to be barely breathing as he watched his husband stare.

"Camden," Lou's voice was small and broken with emotion. "Could I hold her for a minute?"

"You can hold her as long as you want."

By silent agreement, Lou sobbed as Dr. Hampton placed Elisabeth on her chest. They ignored what the doctor and nurses were doing—this was their moment.

"This doesn't get easier. I thought it would after Matty. I understood with Ricky, but it doesn't."

"Lou, no matter what happens, you're her aunt, and when the time comes, she'll know that you gave me and my boys the greatest gift in the fucking world."

"She's beautiful, Lou, thank you," Eric and Ellison said in unison as they leaned into her kissing her cheeks.

The four of them stared down at the slowly calming little girl.

"You never have to say goodbye, but we agreed to your wishes that you wouldn't be around for a while."

"I just need time. I did good, huh?"

He kissed her sweat-dampened hair and held her a little tighter.

"You make some beautiful babies, Lou. You made three families complete, and I won't ever say that I understand the sacrifice you made, but know it's appreciated."

The moment drew out with Lou whispering soft goodbyes and then Carmen came and took Elisabeth away to get her cleaned. Another room was set up for them and Elisabeth. They'd go there and wait for their daughter to come back from the nursery.

"Y'all go on and spend time with your daughter. I need some time alone."

They respected her wishes. He eased from behind her, and he led his husbands out of the room. He glanced back in time to see her break, and when he started to go back to the bed, Carmen was already there. She smiled and shooed them away.

"Will she be okay," Eric asked, his blue eyes filled with tears.

"I'm sure she will, it'll just take time."

"If we'd known—"

"She'll be fine, but she did something extraordinary today and painful. She made a sacrifice, and we'll make sure she always knows she appreciated and welcomed into Elisabeth's life. Let's go to our room and wait for our little girl."

The moment was bittersweet, joy tempered by the misery of another. He was overjoyed about their daughter, but heartbroken by the pain Lou would deal with. She'd kept Elisabeth safe and warm for months, felt every kick and nurtured a life that in the end, she knew she was going to give up. That was an act braver than he'd ever be strong enough to do.

"Eric, Ellison," he said as they stepped into the room and the door closed behind them. They turned to him. "I love you both more than I will ever be able to say."

"You don't have to say it."

"You show us every day."

He kissed his boys while they waited, curled up on the too small bed, and talked about the future and plans. They'd saved his life in more ways than they'd ever understand. They were his everything, and he'd make sure they never regretted being his.

A sweet-faced nurse walked into the room with a beaming smile pulling a bassinet behind her. "Gentlemen, you ready to spend some alone time with your daughter?"

THE END

About the Author

By day, J.M. is an introverted cook hiding out in her kitchen in the middle of nowhere Ohio, by night and any free time she may have, she is a writer of mainly LGBTQ Fiction and Erotica. Although. she's equal opportunity when it comes to telling a story, she'll even write a bit of straight erotic romance when the mood strikes.

She has been writing for years in old notebooks. At the age of eight, she wrote the worst poem in the history of poetry, but it sparked her love for writing. She reads too much and loves to get lost in other worlds and her favorite stories have to include laughter and having the reader doing at least one double take. Thirty-something, forever restless she uses her stories to ground herself, and find her place of peace.

WHERE TO FIND J.M.
www.jmdabneyauthor.com